Pippi

Goes to School

The text in this book has been excerpted, with Astrid Lindgren's assistance, from two chapters of *Pippi Longstocking*.

PUFFIN BOOKS
Published by the Penguin Group
Penguin Putnam Books for Young Readers, 345 Hudson Street, New York, New York 10014, U.S.A.
Penguin Books Ltd, 27 Wrights Lane, London W8 5TZ, England
Penguin Books Australia Ltd, Ringwood, Victoria, Australia
Penguin Books Canada Ltd, 10 Alcorn Avenue, Toronto, Ontario, Canada M4V 3B2
Penguin Books (N.Z.) Ltd, 182-190 Wairau Road, Auckland 10, New Zealand

Penguin Books Ltd, Registered Offices: Harmondsworth, Middlesex, England

Pipi Goes to School first published in the United States of America by Viking,
a member of Penguin Putnam Books for Young Readers, 1998
Published in Puffin Books, a member of Penguin Putnam Books for Young Readers, 1999

9 10

Text copyright The Viking Press, Inc., 1950
Copyright renewed Viking Penguin Inc., 1978
Illustrations copyright © Michael Chesworth, 1998
All rights reserved

THE LIBRARY OF CONGRESS HAS CATALOGED THE VIKING EDITION AS FOLLOWS:
Lindgren, Astrid, date
Pippi goes to school / by Astrid Lindgren ;
illustrated by Michael Chesworth ; translated by Frances Lamborn.
p. cm.—(A Pippi Longstocking storybook)
Summary: After Tommy and Annika entice Pippi into going to school,
her first-and-only day there is unlike anything they ever expected.
ISBN 0-670-88075-2 (hc)
[1. First day of school—Fiction. 2. Schools—Fiction. 3. Humorous stories.]
I. Chesworth, Michael, ill. II. Lamborn, Frances. III. Title. IV. Series: Lindgren, Astrid, date.
Pippi Longstocking storybook.
PZ7.L6585Pgf 1998 [E]—dc21 97-51432 CIP AC

Puffin Books ISBN 978-0-14-130236-2

Printed in China

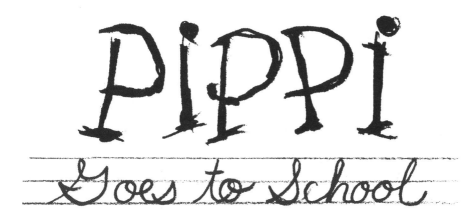

Pippi Goes to School

By Astrid Lindgren
Pictures by Michael Chesworth

PUFFIN BOOKS

Way out at the end of a tiny little town was an old overgrown garden, and in the garden was an old house, and in the house lived Pippi Longstocking. She was nine years old, and she lived there all alone. She had no mother and no father, and that was of course very nice because there was no one to tell her to go to bed just when she was having the most fun, and no one who could make her take cod liver oil when she much preferred caramel candy.

Once upon a time Pippi had had a father of whom she was extremely fond. He was a sea captain who sailed on the great ocean, and Pippi had sailed with him in his ship until one day her father was blown overboard in a storm and disappeared.

But Pippi was absolutely certain he would come back.

Her father had bought the old house in the garden many years ago. While Pippi was waiting for him to come back she went straight home to live at Villa Villekulla. That was the name of the house.

Two things Pippi took with her from the ship: a little monkey whose name was Mr. Nilsson—he was a present from her father—and a big suitcase full of gold pieces. Pippi also had a horse of her own that she had bought with one of her many

gold pieces the day she came home to Villa Villekulla.

Beside Villa Villekulla was another garden and another house. In that house lived a father and mother and two charming children, Tommy and Annika, who often wished for a playmate. And when Pippi Longstocking moved next door, they got the best playmate any child could wish for. This is the story of one of their adventures together. . . .

Of course Tommy and Annika went to school. Each morning at eight o'clock they trotted off, hand in hand, swinging their schoolbags.

At that time Pippi was usually grooming her horse or dressing Mr. Nilsson in his little suit. Or else she was taking her morning exercises, which meant turning forty-three somersaults in a row.

Tommy and Annika always looked longingly toward Villa Villekulla as they started off to school. They would much rather have gone to play with Pippi. If only Pippi had been going to school too; that would have been something else.

The more they thought about it the worse they felt to think that Pippi did not go to school, and at last they determined to try to persuade her to begin.

"You can't imagine what a nice teacher we have," said Tommy artfully to Pippi one afternoon.

"If you only knew what fun it is in school!" Annika added. "I'd die if I couldn't go to school."

Pippi was bathing her feet in a tub.

"You don't have to stay so very long," continued Tommy. "Just until two o'clock."

"Yes, and besides, we get Christmas vacation and Easter vacation and summer vacation," said Annika.

Pippi bit her big toe thoughtfully but still said nothing. Suddenly, she poured all the water out on the kitchen floor, so that Mr. Nilsson, who sat near her playing with a mirror, got his pants absolutely soaked.

"It's not fair!" said Pippi sternly without paying any attention to Mr. Nilsson's puzzled air about his wet pants. "It is absolutely unfair! I don't intend to stand it!"

"What's the matter now?" asked Tommy.

"In four months it will be Christmas, and then you'll have Christmas vacation. But I, what'll I get?" Pippi's voice sounded sad. "No Christmas vacation, not even the tiniest bit of a Christmas vacation," she complained. "Something will have to be done about that. Tomorrow morning I'll begin school."

Tommy and Annika clapped their hands. "Hurrah! We'll wait for you outside our gate at eight o'clock."

"Oh, no," said Pippi. "I can't begin as early as that. And besides, I'm going to ride to school."

And ride she did. Exactly at ten o'clock the next

day she lifted her horse off the porch, and a little later all the people in the town ran to their windows to see what horse it was that was running away.

Pippi galloped wildly into the schoolyard, jumped off the horse, tied him to a tree, and burst into the schoolroom with such a noise and a clatter that

Tommy and Annika and all their classmates jumped
in their seats.

"Hi, there," cried Pippi, waving her big hat.

Tommy and Annika had told their teacher that a
new girl named Pippi Longstocking was coming, and
as she was a very pleasant teacher, she had decided

to do all she could to make Pippi happy in school.

Pippi threw herself down on a vacant bench. The teacher said in a very friendly voice, "Welcome to school, little Pippi. I hope that you will enjoy yourself here and learn a great deal."

"Yes, and I hope I'll get some Christmas vacation," said Pippi. "That is the reason I've come."

"If you would first tell me your whole name," said the teacher, "then I'll register you in school."

"My name is Pippilotta Delicatessa Windowshade Mackrelmint Efraim's Daughter Longstocking, daughter of Captain Efraim Longstocking. Pippi is really only a nickname, because Papa thought that Pippilotta was too long to say."

"Indeed?" said the teacher. "Well, then we shall call you Pippi too. But now," she continued, "suppose we test you a little and see what you know. Let us begin with arithmetic. Pippi, can you tell me what seven plus five is?"

Pippi, astonished and dismayed, looked at her and said, "Well, if you don't know that yourself, you needn't think I'm going to tell you."

15

All the children stared in horror at Pippi, and the teacher explained that one couldn't answer that way in school.

"I beg your pardon," said Pippi contritely. "I didn't know that. I won't do it again."

"No, let us hope not," said the teacher. "And now I will tell you that seven plus five is twelve."

"See that!" said Pippi. "You knew it yourself. Why are you asking then?"

The teacher decided to act as if nothing unusual were happening and went on with her examination.

"Well now, Pippi, how much do you think eight plus four is?"

"Oh, about sixty-seven," hazarded Pippi.

"Of course not," said the teacher. "Eight plus four is twelve."

"Well now, really," said Pippi, "that is carrying things too far. You just said that seven plus five is twelve. There should be some rhyme and reason to things even in school. Furthermore, if you are so childishly interested in that foolishness, why don't you sit down in a corner by yourself and do arithmetic and leave us alone so we can play tag?"

The teacher decided there was no point in trying to teach Pippi any more arithmetic. "Can Tommy answer this one?" she asked. "If Lisa has seven apples and Axel has nine apples, how many apples do they have together?"

"Yes, you tell, Tommy," Pippi interrupted, "and tell

me too, if Lisa gets a stomach-ache and Axel gets more stomach-ache, whose fault is it and where did they get hold of the apples in the first place?"

The teacher tried to pretend that she hadn't heard and turned to Annika. "Now, Annika, here's a problem for you: Gustav was with his schoolmates on a picnic. He had a quarter when he started out and seven cents when he got home. How much did he spend?"

"Yes, indeed," said Pippi, "and I also want to know why he was so extravagant, and if it was pop he bought, and if he washed his ears properly before he left home."

The teacher decided to give up arithmetic altogether. She thought maybe Pippi would prefer to learn to read. So she took out a pretty little card with a picture of an iguana on it. In front of the iguana's nose was the letter "i."

"Now, Pippi," she said briskly, "you'll see something nice. You see here an iguana. And the letter in front of this iguana is called *i*."

"That I'll never believe," said Pippi. "I think it looks exactly like a straight line with a little fly speck over it. But what I'd really like to know is, what has the iguana to do with the fly speck?"

The teacher took out another card with a picture of a snake on it and told Pippi that the letter on that was an *s*.

"Speaking of snakes," said Pippi, "I'll never, ever forget the time I had a fight with a huge snake in India. You can't imagine what a dreadful snake it was, fourteen yards long and mad as a hornet, and one time he came and wanted me for dessert, and he wound himself around me—uhhh!—but I've been around a bit, I said, and hit him in the head, bang, and then I hit him again, and bingo! he was dead, and, indeed, so that is the letter *s*—most remarkable!"

Pippi had to stop to get her breath. And the teacher, who had now begun to think that Pippi was an unruly and troublesome child, decided that the class should have drawing for a while. She took out paper and pencils and passed them out to the children.

"Now you may draw whatever you wish," she said and sat down at her desk and began to correct homework. In a little while she looked up to see how the drawing was going. All the children sat looking at Pippi, who lay flat on the floor, drawing to her heart's content.

"But, Pippi," said the teacher impatiently, "why in the world aren't you drawing on your paper?"

"I filled that long ago. There isn't room enough for my whole horse on that little snip of a paper," said Pippi. "Just now I'm working on his front legs, but when I get to his tail I guess I'll have to go out in the hall."

The teacher thought hard for a while. "Suppose instead we all sing a little song," she suggested.

All the children stood up by their seats except Pippi; she stayed where she was on the floor. "You go ahead and sing," she said. "I'll rest myself a while. Too much learning tires even the healthiest."

But now the teacher's patience came to an end. She told all the children to go out into the yard so she could talk to Pippi alone.

When the teacher and Pippi were alone, Pippi got up and walked to the desk. "Do you know what?" she

said. "It was awfully fun to come to school to find out what it was like. But I don't think I care about going to school any more, Christmas vacation or no Christmas vacation. There's altogether too many apples and iguanas and snakes and things like that. It makes me dizzy in the head. I hope that you, Teacher, won't be sorry."

But the teacher said she certainly was sorry, most of all because Pippi wouldn't behave decently; and that any girl who acted as badly as Pippi did

wouldn't be allowed to go to school even if she wanted to ever so much.

"Have I behaved badly?" asked Pippi, much astonished. "Goodness, I didn't know that," she added. She stood silent for a while, and then she said in a trembling voice, "You understand, Teacher, don't you, that when you have a mother who's an angel and a father who is a cannibal king, and when you have sailed on the ocean all your whole life, then you don't know just how to behave in school with all the apples and iguanas."

Then the teacher said she understood and didn't feel annoyed with Pippi any longer, and maybe Pippi could come back to school when she was a little older. Pippi positively beamed with delight. "I think you are awfully nice, Teacher. And here is something for you."

Out of her pocket Pippi took a lovely little gold watch and laid it on the desk. The teacher said she couldn't possibly accept such a valuable gift from Pippi, but Pippi replied, "You've got to take it; other-

wise I'll come back again tomorrow, and that would be a pretty how-do-you-do."

Then Pippi rushed out to the schoolyard and jumped on her horse. All the children gathered around to pat the horse and see her off.

"You ought to know about the schools in Argentina," said Pippi. "Easter vacation begins three days after Christmas vacation ends, and when Easter vacation is over there are three days and then it's summer vacation. Summer vacation ends on the first of November, and then you have a tough time until Christmas vacation begins on November eleventh. But you can stand that because there are at least no lessons. Arithmetic they don't have at all, and if there is any kid who knows what seven plus five is he has to stand in the corner all day—that is, if he's foolish enough to let the teacher know that he knows. They have reading on Friday, and then only if they have some books, which they never have."

"But what do they do in school?" asked one little boy.

"Eat caramels," said Pippi decidedly. "There is a long pipe that goes from a caramel factory nearby directly into the schoolroom, and caramels keep shooting out of it all day long so the children have all they can do to eat them up."

"Yes, but what does the teacher do?" asked one little girl.

"Takes the paper off the caramels for the children, of course," said Pippi. Then she waved her big hat.

"So long, kids," she cried gaily. "Now you won't see

me for a while. But always remember how many apples Axel had or you'll be sorry."

With a ringing laugh Pippi rode out through the gate so wildly that the pebbles whirled around the horse's hoofs and the windowpanes rattled in the schoolhouse.

P9-DIY-122

TRIBUNE TOWER

AMERICAN LANDMARK

HISTORY, ARCHITECTURE AND DESIGN

COMMENTARY BY BLAIR KAMIN
Chicago Tribune Architecture Critic
and winner of the Pulitzer Prize for criticism

MAJOR PHOTOGRAPHY BY BOB FILA
Chicago Tribune Photographer and winner
of the Pulitzer Prize for explanatory reporting
as a member of the Tribune staff

DRAMATIC DOORWAY The main entrance to Tribune Tower is a masterwork of neo-Gothic art, consisting of an arched portal that surrounds a stone screen portraying the fables of Aesop. The keystone of the arch is made of gray and pink granite. To the left of the arch, a few feet above the Tower's cornerstone, is carved a quotation from the poet John Milton: "Give me liberty to know, to utter and to argue freely according to my conscience, above all other liberties."

VISITOR INFORMATION
Offices and other facilities above Tribune Tower's ground floor are not open to the public, but
the Tower's main lobby can be viewed seven days a week, 24 hours a day.

A Landmark Is Born

Even in Chicago, a city bursting with great buildings, Tribune Tower stands out—a flamboyant, arresting and, in many ways, incomparable skyscraper. Decades after it threw open its doors on July 6, 1925, the 36-story castle of limestone is every bit the civic monument its creators wanted it to be, a uniquely American fusion of the medieval and the modern. Other office buildings—Sears Tower, to name the most obvious—are taller, but few etch such a spectacular silhouette on the skyline or present such a welcoming face to the passerby. And none of them can claim, as this one can, to be the product of one of the most influential architecture competitions in history.

Designed by New York City architects John Mead Howells and Raymond M. Hood, Tribune Tower is both an official Chicago landmark and a landmark in the less formal, everyday meaning of that word. Along with the neighboring Wrigley Building, it forms a grand gateway to one of the world's great shopping streets, North Michigan Avenue. Visitors and Chicagoans alike are delighted by the base of the skyscraper, which is studded with fragments of famous buildings and historic structures. In an age of cheaply constructed, cookie-cutter buildings, Tribune Tower is an extraordinary exception, sending a powerful message about architecture's ability to create both a sense of permanence and a distinct presence amid the blur of city life. Certainly, no other American newspaper is so closely identified with the building that houses it.

Tribune Tower Building
John M. Howells, Raymond M. Hood,
Associated Architects,
Hegeman-Harris Company, Inc.
Photographed by Eugene Cour.

TRANSFORMING TRADITION Tribune Tower was based on Gothic cathedrals but was not a slavish copy. Architects John Mead Howells and Raymond M. Hood took medieval forms and turned them into a modern office building nearly twice as tall as the church towers from which it drew inspiration. The distinctive skyline silhouette of their design is apparent in these photographs, which show a growing steel frame being sheathed in Indiana limestone.

THE CLIENTS *Chicago Tribune* co-editors and co-publishers Joseph M. Patterson (left) and Robert R. McCormick (in light-colored suit) lead the corner-stone-laying ceremony for the newspaper's printing plant. The plant was built in 1920, just to the east of the site where Tribune Tower would be completed in 1925.

THE CLIENTS *Chicago Tribune* co-editors and co-publishers Joseph M. Patterson (left) and Robert R. McCormick (in light-colored suit) lead the corner-stone-laying ceremony for the newspaper's printing plant. The plant was built in 1920, just to the east of the site where Tribune Tower would be completed in 1925.

ROBERT R. McCORMICK

JOSEPH M. PATTERSON

Stepping into the Tower's hushed, churchlike lobby or looking at the strange carvings that decorate its exterior walls, visitors can sense the almost-religious spirit that animated its builders. The phrase "Cathedral of Commerce" was coined for an earlier neo-Gothic skyscraper, the Woolworth Building in New York City, but it seems made to order for the Tower, a hymn in stone to truth, beauty, the heroes of war and the highest ideals of journalism.

It is no accident that Tribune Tower speaks with such a strong, and at times idiosyncratic, voice. While today's office buildings are shaped by cautious committees and penny-pinching efficiency experts, the Tower was built during an era when a single individual could stamp a building with his unmistakable imprint.

In the Tower's case, there were two visionaries, *Chicago Tribune* co-editors and co-publishers Col. Robert R. McCormick and Capt. Joseph M. Patterson. Veterans of World War I, as well as grandsons of the great *Tribune* editor Joseph Medill, McCormick and Patterson were a classic odd couple. McCormick was well dressed and aristocratic, retaining a slight British accent from his childhood years in England. Patterson was a rumpled-looking populist who, even though he was every bit as wealthy as McCormick, enjoyed mingling with common people. In 1925, Patterson left Chicago to run the tabloid *Daily News* in New York City, putting the *Chicago Tribune* solely under McCormick's control. The Colonel, as McCormick was popularly known, would rise to national prominence in the 1930s as a fierce

Where World's Most Beautiful Building Will Stand

This photo shows the vacant site immediately in front of The Tribune plant at Michigan and Austin avenues upon which a new building is to be erected. It is for an architectural design for this structure that The Tribune inaugurated a $100,000 contest. To win the prize the architect must make a design of the most beautiful building in the modern world. Already architects from all parts of the world have signified their intention of entering the contest. This vacant area shown in the photo comprises 13,500 square feet. To the south and west it overlooks the river and the commercial heart of Chicago; to the north and east it faces the parks and drives and Lake Michigan.

NO LITTLE PLANS On its 75th anniversary, the *Chicago Tribune* announced an international architecture competition for its new Michigan Avenue headquarters (right). A 1922 photograph (above) showed the planned location of Tribune Tower in front of the *Chicago Tribune's* printing plant.

$100,000.00

IN PRIZES TO ARCHITECTS

Seventy-five years old today, The Tribune seeks surpassing beauty in new home on Michigan Boulevard

THE TRIBUNE herewith offers $100,000.00 in prizes for designs for a building to be erected on its vacant lot at North Michigan Boulevard and Austin Avenue. Commemoration of our Seventy-fifth Birthday is made in this manner for three reasons:

—to adorn with a monument of enduring beauty this city, in which The Tribune has prospered so amazingly.

—to create a structure which will be an inspiration and a model for generations of newspaper publishers.

—to provide a new and beautiful home worthy of the world's greatest newspaper.

The contest will be under the rules of the American Institute of Architects. Competition will be open and international. Each competitor will be required to submit drawings showing the west and south elevations and perspective from the southwest, of a new building to be erected on The Tribune's property at the corner of North Michigan Blvd. and Austin Ave. Architects desiring complete information are requested to write to

Robert R. McCormick, Joseph M. Patterson, Editors and Publishers

The Chicago Tribune
The World's Greatest Newspaper

SEVENTY-FIVE YEARS OLD TODAY

opponent of Franklin D. Roosevelt's New Deal and of American involvement in World War II.

Whatever their differences in personal style and career trajectory, McCormick and Patterson apparently did not know the meaning of the word scrimp; to the Colonel, in particular, nothing was too good for the *Chicago Tribune* or for Chicago. On opening day in 1925, his newspaper bragged in a front-page story that Tribune Tower had cost $8.5 million, easily exceeding the cost per cubic foot of any other skyscraper in the world.

Now the headquarters of Tribune Company, which has grown to be a leading media company with operations in television and radio broadcasting, publishing and interactive ventures, Tribune Tower is all the more remarkable when it is compared with the *Chicago Tribune's* first home: a third-floor loft in a humble wood building on the southwest corner of LaSalle and Lake Streets. There, on June 10, 1847, the first 400 copies of the newspaper were printed on a hand press.

In time, the *Chicago Tribune* would thrust its journalistic roots deep into the soil of the city and become a powerful force in the Midwest. By 1902, the growing newspaper built its own 18-story office building on the southeast corner of Dearborn and Madison Streets. Then, in 1920, the *Tribune* put up a new printing plant in a former bean field on the north bank of the Chicago River.

The plant was set back from Michigan Avenue in anticipation of the day when a Tribune skyscraper would be built out front. It was dismal territory

HOMES OF THE CHICAGO TRIBUNE

1847
LaSalle and Lake Streets

1849
Clark and Randolph Streets

1850
171½ Lake Street

1872
Dearborn and Madison Streets

1902
Dearborn and Madison Streets

A CARTOONIST'S WHIMSY
In the competition entry of *Tribune* cartoonist Carey Orr, Tribune Tower was portrayed as a man with a clothespin on his nose—avoiding the smell from the neighboring soap factory.

THE HEIGHT OF SELF-PROMOTION
The design of *Tribune* cartoonist Gaar Williams put in a plug for cartoonists— "More Art," said the motto near the summit of Tribune Tower.

back then, lined by a soap factory, billboards and saloons. But McCormick and Patterson had a grand vision.

To mark the *Chicago Tribune's* 75th anniversary of publishing on June 10, 1922, they announced an international competition for the design of Tribune Tower. To quash any doubts about their seriousness and to lure talented architects, they put up $100,000 in prize money. Their goal: "To erect the most beautiful and distinctive office building in the world."

Hyperbole had long been one of the *Chicago Tribune's* characteristics. It billed itself as the "World's Greatest Newspaper," a risky piece of self-labeling at best. And now it mandated a skyscraper whose beauty would have no equal, a building that would promote the newspaper and erase Chicago's old image as a rube town skilled mostly at butchering hogs. There was considerable skepticism about all this. Some called it mere puffery.

But then the designs came pouring in: 263 of them from 23 countries. They still represent an astonishing assortment of approaches to the skyscraper, a perfect snapshot of where the art of architecture stood in the 1920s and an equally accurate gauge of where it was going.

One of the foreign proposals, from architects Walter Gropius and Adolf Meyer, reflected the industrial aesthetic then being taught at the Bauhaus, the avant-garde design school in Weimar, Germany. In retrospect, it seems prophetic, signaling the coming dominance of steel-and-glass modernism after the Second World War.

Another entry, by Czech-born Adolf Loos, envisioned Tribune Tower as an oversized Doric column standing atop a boxy base that resembled a platform. Some have dismissed the design as a phallic joke, but maybe it wasn't. Historians have speculated that the classical column symbolized a newspaper column. The platform-like base may have suggested a raised seating area in a church, which happens to be called a tribune.

While many of the foreign entries looked to the future, their American counterparts borrowed freely from the past. There were skyscrapers topped by classical temples, domes, pyramids and obelisks. One proposal even called for topping the Tower with a sculpture of a Roman tribune—not a bad symbol for a mass-circulation newspaper, given that in ancient Rome, a tribune was a magistrate who protected the interests and rights of the plebeians from the patricians.

Joining the visual feast, the *Chicago Tribune's* three editorial cartoonists lampooned the seriousness of the competition with their own whimsical entries. Cartoonist Carey Orr depicted the newspaper's new home as a man with a clothespin on his nose. Poking fun at Tribune Tower's odoriferous environs, Orr drew a mock sign in front of his newspaper building that deadpanned: "Our Neighbors—The Kirk Soap Works."

If the competition had been held at the high tide of modern architecture in the 1950s, the modern vision probably would have won out. But in 1922, the *Tribune's* conservative Midwestern jury wasn't ready for the Bauhaus.

THE ARCHITECTS

The architects who won first, second and third prizes in the Tribune Tower competition were among the leading designers of the 20th Century.

FIRST PLACE

JOHN MEAD HOWELLS   Born in 1868 in Cambridge, Massachusetts. Son of American novelist and *Atlantic Monthly* editor William Dean Howells. Educated at Massachusetts Institute of Technology and Harvard University, from which he graduated in 1891. Earned diploma at the Ecole des Beaux Arts in Paris in 1897. Practiced in New York City. Teamed with Raymond M. Hood for the Tribune Tower competition. Notable works included Beekman Tower in New York City, buildings for Harvard, Yale and Columbia Universities, as well as buildings for bank and trust companies in New York City, San Francisco and Seattle. Also designed the Daily News Building (1930) in New York City with Hood. Died in 1959.

JOHN MEAD HOWELLS

RAYMOND M. HOOD   Born in 1881 in Pawtucket, Rhode Island. Studied at Brown University and graduated from Massachusetts Institute of Technology in 1903. Obtained diploma from Ecole des Beaux Arts in Paris before returning to United States in 1911. Designed several New York City skyscrapers after winning Tribune Tower competition. Key projects included the American Radiator Building, with Godley and Fouilhoux (1924); the Daily News Building, with Howells (1930); Rockefeller Center, with Reinhard and Hofmeister, Godley and Fouilhoux, Corbett and Harrison (1931-39); and the McGraw-Hill Building, with Fouilhoux (1931). Also designed the General Electric Pavilion at the 1933 Century of Progress Exposition in Chicago. Died in 1934.

RAYMOND M. HOOD

SECOND PLACE

ELIEL SAARINEN   Born in 1873 in Rantasalmi, Finland. Used $20,000 second-place prize money from Tribune Tower competition to move to the United States in 1923. Lived briefly in Evanston, then moved to Ann Arbor, where he taught at the University of Michigan. Later settled in Bloomfield Hills, Michigan, where he played a leading role in the planning and design of Cranbrook, a renowned art and architecture school. Was Cranbrook's resident architect from 1925 to 1950 and president of its Academy of Art from 1932 to 1946. Teamed with his son, Eero, and the Chicago firm of Perkins, Wheeler and Will to design the innovative and influential Crow Island Elementary School in Winnetka (1940). Died in 1950.

ELIEL SAARINEN

THIRD PLACE

HOLABIRD & ROCHE   Firm established in 1883 by William Holabird, born in 1854 in Armenia Union, New York, and Martin Roche, born in 1853 in Cleveland. At time of the Tribune competition, other partners were Edward Renwick; Holabird's son, John A. Holabird; and John W. Root, son of John W. Root of the Chicago firm Burnham & Root. Firm's significant Chicago-area works included Ft. Sheridan (1890, 1892), the south end of the Monadnock Building (1893), the Old Colony Building (1894), the Marquette Building (1895), the Chicago Tribune Building at Dearborn and Madison Streets (1902), the Cook County Courthouse-Chicago City Hall (1910) and Soldier Field (1926). William Holabird died in 1923, Roche in 1927.

WILLIAM HOLABIRD   MARTIN ROCHE

The winning design by John Mead Howells and Raymond M. Hood of New York City was a study in uninterrupted vertical lines, its bands of limestone rising straight up to the building's summit. After the Howells and Hood entry was selected, the *Chicago Tribune* added four floors to the building, creating more rentable office space and markedly improving upon the proportions of the original design.

The designs came pouring in. They still represent an astonishing assortment of approaches to the skyscraper, a perfect snapshot of where the art of architecture stood in the 1920s and an equally accurate gauge of where it was going.

Left
SECOND PLACE
The entry by Finnish architect Eliel Saarinen turned out to be the Tribune competition's most influential design, its trim vertical look defining American skyscrapers from Chicago's Palmolive Building to the RCA Building in New York City's Rockefeller Center. The great Chicago architect Louis Sullivan called it "a voice, resonant and rich, ringing amidst the wealth and joy of life."

Right
THIRD PLACE
The eclectic proposal by Chicago architects Holabird & Roche had neo-Gothic elements like those of the winner and street-level arches comparable to those of the second-place finisher. Holabird & Roche already had worked for the *Chicago Tribune,* having designed the newspaper's 1902 Loop headquarters at Dearborn and Madison Streets.

Left
PROPHET OF MODERNISM
Walter Gropius and Adolf Meyer of Weimar, Germany, anticipated the steel and glass high-rises that would dominate American architecture after World War II. But in 1922, the Tribune's conservative Midwestern jury wasn't ready for the Bauhaus.

Right
NEWSPAPER COLUMN
The design by Adolf Loos of Nice, France, with its thrusting Doric column, was long regarded as a phallic joke. In recent years, however, architectural historians have wondered if Loos should be credited for a more subtle, symbolic exercise. Could the classical column have suggested a newspaper column?

BOMBAST FROM THE PAST
Most of the entries in the Tribune
competition looked to the past for
inspiration, none more so than the
design by Saverio Dioguardi of Italy,
with its overblown reference to Roman
triumphal arches. The ball-like form
atop his tower would be repeated in
another skyscraper near Tribune Tower
—see photograph on Page 13.

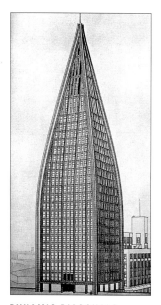

DYNAMIC DIAGONALS
The Tribune contest featured many
radical modern proposals, such as this
powerfully geometric design by Bruno
Taut, Walter Gunther and Kurz Schutz
of Germany. It looks forward to a later
phase of modernism, when architects
broke out of the glass box and turned
their towers into giant abstract sculptures.

Howells and Hood, who based Tribune Tower on Gothic cathedrals in France and Belgium, won the first prize of $50,000. An innovative skyscraper plan by Finnish architect Eliel Saarinen took the $20,000 second prize. And an eclectic entry from the Chicago firm of Holabird & Roche, designers of the *Tribune's* earlier 18-story office building, won the $10,000 third prize.

Ironically, the proposal by Saarinen, who had never before designed a skyscraper, turned out to be more influential than the winner. Saarinen's tower had the same telescoping profile as many of the American designs, but rose more gracefully because of its refined setbacks and delicate vertical projections. It also was more abstract than Howells and Hood's heavily ornamented high-rise, striking a balance between the modern aesthetic of the Europeans and the traditional look of the Americans.

The great Chicago architect Louis Sullivan called it "a voice, resonant and rich, ringing amidst the wealth and joy of life." In the next two decades, its trim vertical look would become a model, defining the profiles of American skyscrapers from Chicago's Palmolive Building to the RCA Building in New York City's Rockefeller Center. Yet it still did not beat the design by Howells and Hood.

For years, critics of the Tribune competition lamented this outcome, echoing Sullivan's view that the winning entry represented "dying ideas" while Saarinen's was "a priceless pearl." There also were rumblings that Howells and Hood had an inside track because Howells' wife was the daughter of former *Chicago Tribune* editor Horace White, who led the newspaper from 1866 to 1874. But in recent years, both Tribune Tower and the Tribune competition have been portrayed in a far more favorable light.

"The *Tribune* wanted the best building going," the dean of American architectural historians, Yale University's Vincent Scully, wrote in 1980. "Expense was no object. It ran an honest competition and built the winner by Howells and Hood. Some may have felt that Eliel Saarinen's design was even better, but it is impossible to really fault the choice. Raymond Hood went on to become the greatest skyscraper architect of all time."

Howells and Hood were as much a study in contrasts as their clients. Howells, the son of American novelist William Dean Howells, was older and more established; he teamed with Hood for the Tribune competition because the younger man had demonstrated a talent for winning design contests. Nonetheless, Hood was so poor at the time that, when the pair won the Tribune competition, he had to borrow money to buy a suitable coat before attending the awards ceremony. Hood clearly was the lesser known of the duo. The *Chicago Tribune* headline on Dec. 3, 1922, read: "Howells Wins in Contest for Tribune Tower." Hood wasn't mentioned until the second paragraph.

Framed in steel and clad in Indiana limestone, Tribune Tower follows the standard skyscraper model of the 1920s. Its top and bottom are heavily decorated, separated by a relatively austere middle. But the way this formula

is carried out is anything but conventional, from the ornately carved arch that frames the building's entrance to the ring of flying buttresses that are its most distinctive feature.

The architects took superb advantage of the Tower's prominent site, which allows it to be seen from all four sides. The skyscraper's corners are sliced on a diagonal, not squared off, as is typical in such buildings. The Tower tapers gracefully, especially in its upper reaches, rather than resembling a set of boxes piled on one another, as many skyscrapers of its era did. Its top is eight-sided—almost round—a pointed departure from the norm in Chicago, where the right angle is king. With these elements, Howells and Hood gave their building a powerful sculptural presence, as if it were a hunk of clay molded by an artist's hands.

But unlike clay, the Tower is anything but earthbound. Instead, it seems propelled into the sky both by its overall shape and by a range of skillfully handled details. Bands of limestone, or piers, project slightly beyond the windows, creating uninterrupted vertical lines. The windows themselves achieve the same effect, culminating in tall, thin arches. Then there are the flying buttresses, which link the blocky midsection of the skyscraper with the architectural pyrotechnics at the top. As a result, the piers rush straight up to the building's summit, and the skyscraper, despite its weighty limestone

BOUL MICH GLORY
In the 1920s, a parade of skyscrapers transformed once-utilitarian Michigan Avenue into an elegant business district. Viewed from the northwest, left to right, are the Medinah Athletic Club (now the InterContinental Chicago hotel), Tribune Tower and the Wrigley Building. Across the river, also left to right, are 333 N. Michigan Ave., the London Guarantee & Accident Building (now 360 N. Michigan Ave.) and the partially obscured Mather Tower (now 75 E. Wacker Dr.). Still, workaday uses persisted—note the factory smokestacks to Tribune Tower's south.

THE GARDEN, NOT THE MACHINE
The architects of Tribune Tower were influenced by the Arts and Crafts movement of design, which reacted against the standardization of industrial production and celebrated the infinite variety of nature. As a result, the Tower's decoration depicts plant, animal and insect life, including this sculpted bumblebee hovering above the main entrance.

PATRIOTIC DISPLAY
Tribune Tower featured the finest materials, even in the panels beneath its windows, which were made of lead. Making a patriotic statement, the decoration of some panels depicted the American eagle (above) and the five-pointed American star. Others, in a reference to the *Tribune's* name, featured the fasces and the ax, symbols of the authority of the Roman tribunes.

cladding, appears ready to lift off the ground like a rocket. It certainly seems taller than its height of 456 feet—rather modest when compared with Sears Tower's 1,450 feet.

"We feel that in this design we have produced a unit," Howells said in a 1922 speech. "It is not a tower or top placed on a building. It is all one building. It will climb into the air naturally."

To be sure, there are weaknesses. The buttresses make the Tower look somewhat top-heavy and, moreover, they don't hold up anything, as their medieval predecessors did. They're merely decorative—"stage scenery to the last degree," as one critic said. But what a stage set this is. In contrast to the vast majority of office buildings, which are a solid mass, the arching cut-outs formed by the buttresses allow passersby to actually see through the building. In effect, they put the sky within the skyscraper.

The Tower also distinguishes itself through its skillful interplay of opposites. Strong features, such as the buttresses, accentuate the delicate features, such as the open Gothic tracery, and vice versa. Adding to the drama: the floodlighting that Howells and Hood provided for the building's summit. Illuminated against the night sky, the Tower's finials, flying buttresses and open tracery suggest a softly glowing crown.

As the Art Institute of Chicago commented in "The Sky's the Limit," a 1990 book about Chicago skyscrapers, the Tower "has an unsurpassed visual presence on the skyline."

While alluring from a distance, Tribune Tower is equally appealing from up close. It's no one-liner that knocks the viewer's eyes out with a dazzling silhouette, then has nothing else to say. It breaks down into clearly recognizable parts that enrich the whole, including a 22-story "bustle" that projects from its eastern end. The bustle, which creates additional office space on the middle and lower floors, is joined to the Tower proper by a fire escape, surely the only one of its kind topped by a mansard roof.

Other touches enhance the Tower's ability to work on a human scale while leavening its almost overwhelming seriousness. Among them is an intricate limestone screen, framed by the building's grand entrance arch, which features figures from Aesop's fables. In the tradition of medieval masons who left cartoon-like carvings of themselves on the great cathedrals, Howells and Hood created whimsical self-images in the screen. Howells is represented by a dog emitting howls, Hood by a figure of Robin Hood.

The most pedestrian-friendly features of all are the nearly 150 fragments of famous buildings and historic sites, including the Great Wall of China, the Parthenon and the Taj Mahal, that are embedded in the building's base. On a given day, knots of tourists run their hands across them or pose for pictures in front of them. It's details like these that make the Tower seem powerful, but not monolithic; impressive, but approachable.

To their considerable credit, Howells and Hood weren't content to make the skyscraper an object preening in isolation; the Tower works beautifully in

concert with its neighbors. Along with the Spanish Revival Wrigley Building of 1922, it strongly defines the entrance to the shopping district of North Michigan Avenue—and does much more. The Tribune-Wrigley duo is actually the northern half of a superb quartet of towers. South of the Michigan Avenue bridge, another pairing is formed by the stepped-back Art Deco sliver known as 333 N. Michigan Ave., completed in 1928, and the bowed, neoclassical building at 360 N. Michigan Ave. (called the London Guarantee & Accident Building when it was finished in 1923). While each of these buildings makes a potent statement of its own, they together engage in a memorable visual conversation, forming one of the nation's greatest ensembles of 1920s skyscrapers.

In addition to its handsome form, Tribune Tower was designed with an eye toward function. Its steel frame was an impressive work of structural engineering. By the standards of the 1920s, its floor plan provided an abundance of column-free office space. Along with the *Chicago Tribune* newsroom, printing presses and offices for both Tribune Company and its tenants, the Tower housed a post office, two telegraph stations and numerous shops. It was, according to a 1930s guidebook, a veritable city in miniature—one that consumed 1.2 million gallons of water annually, used 18,000 electric lights and had 5,000 motors operated by push-button control.

CITADEL OF THE FOURTH ESTATE
The flying buttresses of Tribune Tower gave the building symbolic power as well as visual punch. Suggesting the battlements of a castle, they evoked the journalistic imperative to battle for the truth. The *Tribune* even referred to the building's design as "military Gothic." Such symbolism also would have had personal meaning. McCormick and Patterson had just returned to Chicago from the World War I battlefields of Europe. Now they were fighting corruption and waging other journalistic battles on their home turf.

ARCHITECTURAL ALLUSIONS
In 1980, Chicago architects Stuart Cohen and Stanley Tigerman organized "Late Entries to the Chicago Tribune Tower Competition." Many of the designs were in-jokes, like this one by Boston architect Fred Koetter. Referring to the original entry by German architects Walter Gropius and Adolf Meyer, it suggested the downfall of modernism.

MODERN CLASSICISM
A "Late Entries" design by Robert A.M. Stern used the proposal from Adolf Loos in the original competition as a takeoff point, envisioning a classical tower made of glass. It paved the way for columnar skyscrapers that actually were built in the 1980s, including Kevin Roche's Leo Burnett Building at 35 W. Wacker Dr. in Chicago.

Despite the Tower's glories, its architectural reputation temporarily dropped during the 1950s and 1960s. Modern architects of the steel-and-glass school of design disdained the Tower's ornamentation and buttresses. But things came full circle in the 1980s with the rise of a new approach to architecture: postmodernism. Rejecting sterile city centers by the likes of Ludwig Mies van der Rohe and his followers, postmodernism instead looked favorably on skyscrapers that reflected styles from the past and added romance to the skyline.

In Chicago, the postmodern movement was led by a group of maverick architects who called themselves "the Chicago Seven." In 1980, some of these rebels organized an exhibition called "Late Entries to the Chicago Tribune Tower Competition." Their ostensible purpose was to take the pulse of architecture in the 1980s, much as the original competition had done in the 1920s.

There were major differences, however. The chief ones were that no winners would be selected and no skyscraper built. That gave the 1980 postmodern entries a feeling of fantasy. Many of them were simply architectural in-jokes.

The collapsing tower of Boston architect Fred Koetter looked back to the original competition entry by Gropius and Meyer, underscoring the death of the Bauhaus style. Robert A.M. Stern of New York City used Loos' skyscraper-as-column design as a takeoff point for a foray into postmodern classicism. Chicago's Helmut Jahn produced a spectacular new Tower that leaped up from the original. Frank Gehry of California sent in a half-hearted doodle.

The critics were underwhelmed. Compared with the gorgeous, full-bodied drawings of the 1922 competition, those of the "Late Entries" seemed, at best, slick and, at worst, feeble.

"The new competition, like the old, represents a kind of watershed in taste, a moment of vision and decision," Scully commented. "The old one made everyone realize that their present was great. The present one suggests that our past was better."

Meanwhile, the 1922 competition continued to inspire serious architecture. Later in the 1980s, Connecticut architect Cesar Pelli paid tribute to Saarinen's second-place entry with a setback skyscraper, known by its address, at 181 W. Madison St. At the same time, Skidmore, Owings & Merrill of Chicago included buttresses in Chicago's NBC Tower, echoing one of the major features of the nearby Tribune. As if to cap Tribune Tower's comeback, the building was added in 1989 to Chicago's list of architectural landmarks.

Today, the Tower has taken on the iconic status of the very building fragments that stud its base. If it once symbolized the progress of a city on the make, it now represents stability in an ever-shifting world. If it once seemed overly traditional, it now shows that the past should be part of the future. More than ever, it stands as a quintessential American creation, representing the quest to achieve a sense of permanence—and pride of place—by transforming monuments from the Old World into landmarks for a restless young nation.

Fragments of History

However spectacular the crown of Tribune Tower may be, one of the quirkiest and most beloved features of the skyscraper is found at street level: nearly 150 fragments of famous structures and historic sites from around the world and all 50 states. Embedded in the Tower's first-story walls, the stones include chunks of the Great Wall of China, the Great Pyramid of Cheops, and such historic American buildings as the Alamo.

Far from being a mere curiosity, however, these bits and pieces of history speak volumes about the oversized aspirations of Tribune Tower's creators: to make their fledgling skyscraper one of the world's great monuments. As architecture historian Katherine Solomonson has written, the Tower doesn't simply stand among the major buildings of the past; "it stands *upon* them—quite literally."

In this, as in all aspects of the Tower, it's easy to see the hand of Col. Robert R. McCormick, the *Chicago Tribune's* longtime editor and publisher. The tradition of displaying the stones began in 1914, almost by accident when McCormick was covering World War I for the *Tribune.* Touring a medieval cathedral in Ypres, Belgium, that had been damaged by German shelling, he grabbed a fragment for himself.

The Colonel later instructed his correspondents to obtain more stones during their overseas assignments. He insisted that the reporters gather these rocks "by honorable means." But faced with the choice of displeasing their boss or being less than honorable, some invariably chose the latter, as *Tribune* staff writer Ron Grossman has reported. Shipping a stone from St. Peter's to Chicago, the *Tribune's* Rome correspondent, David Darrah,

TOURISTS' DELIGHT
Children from a Milwaukee youth group inspect the stone from Abraham Lincoln's birthplace during a 1956 visit.

SET IN STONE
A crowd gathers in front of Tribune Tower in 1933 for the dedication of a stone from the Alamo. Many Texans in Chicago for the World's Fair attended the event.

GLOBAL ROCK COLLECTING
During his U.S. Army service in World War I, *Tribune* editor and publisher Robert R. McCormick started the collection of stones that stud the base of Tribune Tower; later, he instructed his network of foreign correspondents to expand the collection—only "by honorable means." Here, in 1924, the *Tribune's* Near East correspondent, Raymond Fendrick, secures a stone from the Parthenon in Athens.

A WALK ON THE MOON
This fist-sized, 3.4-billion-year-old moon rock was gathered during the Apollo 15 mission and originally put on display to commemorate the 30th anniversary of the first lunar landing in 1969. On long-term loan from the National Aeronautics and Space Administration, it is exhibited in a bulletproof case set into the wall near Tribune Tower's main entrance.

informed McCormick that it had been procured from the Pope's apartment "due to the fact that repairs were being made."

Some *Tribune* staff members—including William L. Shirer, who would become a distinguished historian of Nazi Germany—encountered resistance while on rock-collecting duty. A member of the newspaper's Paris bureau in the 1920s, Shirer was sent to Rouen, France, site of a medieval cathedral tower that helped inspire Tribune Tower. Word of his assignment, it turned out, had preceded him. "I arrived one morning in Rouen," Shirer recalled, "and picked up the paper and there was a huge banner line across the whole front page: '*Chicago Tribune* correspondent arrives in Rouen to steal a stone from our beloved Cathedral.'" In fact, the *Tribune's* records appear to show that a fragment from the church was properly obtained and shipped to Chicago in 1928.

Eventually, fragments from more than 30 countries would be brought to the Tower. Among the collection's highlights are pieces from the ceiling of the cave in Bethlehem where Jesus is said to have been born. Long displayed in a special case in the Tower's Nathan Hale Lobby, the cave fragments were placed in storage before the lobby was refurbished in 1997. They have been reinstalled in the lobby's west wall.

Major recent acquisitions to the collection include a piece of the Berlin Wall, installed in 1990, and a moon rock, on long-term loan from the National Aeronautics and Space Administration. A special window exhibit for the moon rock was dedicated on July 21, 1999, coinciding with the 30th anniversary of the first manned landing on the moon. In 2002, part of a steel beam from the destroyed World Trade Center in New York was added to the walls of Tribune Tower. It offers a permanent tribute to the victims of the Sept. 11, 2001, terrorist attacks and their families.

While it is easy to think of the stones as an isolated feature of Tribune Tower, they actually make a significant contribution to its form and its meaning. Far from resembling pimples in the Tower's elegant skin of Indiana limestone, the stones are handsome visual accents, their range of colors—reddish-brown, yellow, white, green—enriching the already-varied hues of the building's gray facade. Protruding slightly from the limestone blocks, the fragments also cast beautiful shadow patterns.

Above all, the stones are the star attractions in a popular outdoor historical exhibit that is, at root, a vicarious 'round-the-world tour. They not only demonstrate the global reach of the *Chicago Tribune,* but also bring an exotic flavor to this building in the American heartland.

Ultimately, the stones represent a living record of how McCormick sought to appropriate the power of the ancient wonders of the world to lend authenticity to his brand-new building. That he succeeded is beyond doubt. Just look—set among the stones lining the Tower's Nathan Hale Court is a plaque naming Tribune Tower an official Chicago landmark.

A GUIDE TO THE STONES AND THEIR LOCATIONS

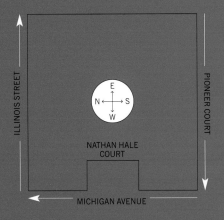

ILLINOIS STREET

PIONEER COURT

NATHAN HALE COURT

MICHIGAN AVENUE

A COMPREHENSIVE TOUR

On the following pages is a guide to the famous stones embedded in the walls of Tribune Tower. It starts at the building's southeast corner, turns north on Michigan Avenue, then east on Illinois Street. Stones may be moved from time to time to allow for new stones or building alterations.

○ = Pictured

PIONEER COURT

Revolutionary War Battlefield, Princeton, New Jersey. On January 3, 1777, ten days after their victory at Trenton, revolutionary troops commanded by George Washington defeated a large British force at Princeton.

Washington's Landing Place, Delaware River, New Jersey. One of the most heroic achievements in America's fight for freedom took place on Christmas night, 1776, when George Washington took his army across the Delaware to launch a surprise attack on the British in New Jersey.

Reims Cathedral, Reims, France. This world-famous Gothic church was begun in 1211 and completed a century later. Many French kings were crowned in it, including Charles VII, whose coronation in 1429 was attended by Joan of Arc.

Revolutionary War Battlefield, Trenton, New Jersey. Less than a day after Washington and his troops crossed the Delaware, they inflicted a heavy defeat on British troops at Trenton. The Americans captured 900 Hessian mercenaries serving with the British.

Pilgrims' Settlement, Leyden, The Netherlands. This was the building occupied for 11 years by the Pilgrim Fathers before sailing on their historic voyage in the Mayflower in 1620.

Quarry, Mount Pentelicus, Greece. Ten miles northeast of Athens are the quarries that provided the pure white marble used in building the temple of Athena—better known as the Parthenon—on the Acropolis of Athens. Work on the temple began in 447 B.C.

○ Fortress Walls, Cartagena, Colombia. This city, founded in 1533, is one of the oldest in the Western Hemisphere. It was attacked and ransacked many times, once by the Elizabethan buccaneer Sir Francis Drake. Its walls, built in the 17th Century, are 50 to 60 feet thick and 40 feet high.

Butter Tower, Cathedral of Notre Dame, Rouen, France. Construction of this magnificent Gothic church began in the 13th Century; the Butter Tower itself was built between 1487 and 1507. It got its name because a papal indulgence permitted people to eat butter during Lent as long as they paid a fine to the building fund. Because of its resemblance in design and general mass to Tribune Tower, the Butter Tower is of special interest to Chicagoans.

○ Mosque of Suleiman the Magnificent, Istanbul, Turkey. Designed by Sinan, Turkey's greatest architect, this mosque was begun in 1549 and completed in 1557. It was built at the command of Suleiman I, sultan of Turkey, 1520-1566, under whose reign Vienna was unsuccessfully besieged in 1529.

○ Steel beam fragment, World Trade Center, New York. This part of a steel beam from the destroyed twin towers was embedded in Tribune Tower as a permanent tribute to the victims of the Sept. 11, 2001, terrorist attacks and their families. Among those killed in the attacks was Steve Jacobson, transmitter maintenance engineer for Tribune Broadcasting's WPIX-TV. He was stationed in the World Trade Center's north tower.

○ Bridge, Forbidden City, Beijing, China. This bridge separated the "Middle Sea" from the "North Sea" in the Forbidden City, the group of imperial buildings, dating from 1421, that includes the emperor's and other palaces, pagodas and museums rich in art treasures.

Battlements of Fortress Ehrenbreitstein, Rhineland, Germany. Across the Rhine from Coblenz, the stronghold was first built in 1128, probably on the site of an earlier fortress. Rebuilt in the 19th Century, it was occupied by American and French troops in 1945.

FORTRESS WALLS
CARTAGENA, COLOMBIA

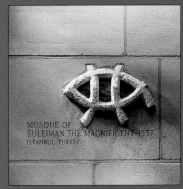

MOSQUE OF SULEIMAN THE MAGNIFICENT
ISTANBUL, TURKEY

STEEL BEAM FRAGMENT
WORLD TRADE CENTER, NEW YORK

BRIDGE
FORBIDDEN CITY, BEIJING, CHINA

SHRINE OF HIBIYA DAIJINGUM
TOKYO, JAPAN

GREAT WALL OF CHINA

BERLIN WALL
GERMANY

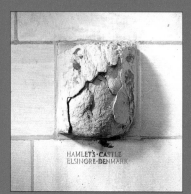

HAMLET'S CASTLE
ELSINORE, DENMARK

Santo Domingo Monastery Church, Panama City, Panama. Built in 1673, this edifice has been in ruins for many years. A unique survivor of the destruction is the famous "flat arch" with a span of 40 feet. Despite having no internal supports, it has withstood fire and earthquake for close to three centuries.

St. Stephen's Cathedral, Vienna, Austria. Its soaring steeple, which has dominated Vienna since the 15th Century, is regarded as one of the masterworks of Central European Gothic architecture.

Abraham Lincoln's Original Tomb, Springfield, Illinois. Designed by Larkin Meade, the original Lincoln tomb was dedicated in 1874. In 1901 it was practically rebuilt using the same materials. A second reconstruction was completed in 1931, and President Herbert Hoover made the dedication speech.

○ Shrine of Hibiya Daijingum, Tokyo, Japan. This stone is from a carved lantern that stood for 600 years in the courtyard of an ancient temple. In the 1860s, it was presented to Hibiya Daijingum, head of the Shinto religion.

Roman ruins, Leptis Magna, Libya. After Roman legions ousted the Carthaginians, Leptis Magna flourished under Roman rule until 455 B.C. when the Vandals invaded. It is now regarded as one of the finest sites for Roman ruins in the Mediterranean.

MICHIGAN AVENUE - SOUTH WING

The Alamo, San Antonio, Texas. "The cradle of Texas liberty," where James Bowie, David Crockett and 185 other heroic defenders died when the fort was besieged by the Mexican general Santa Anna in 1836.

Cathedral, Trondheim, Norway. Considered the finest ecclesiastical structure in Norway, Trondheim Cathedral was where all Norwegian kings were crowned. It dates from about 1200.

Wartburg Castle, near Eisenach, Germany. This famous castle, built in the last half of the 11th Century, was where Martin Luther was brought for protection by the Elector of Saxony in 1521. Here, Luther completed his translation of the New Testament into German.

○ Great Wall of China. This unique structure, 1,500 miles long and averaging 25 feet in height, was begun in 214 B.C. as a defense against invasion by Tartar tribes. The stone in Tribune Tower is from the section in Nankow Pass, about 40 miles northwest of Beijing.

○ Berlin Wall, Germany. The jagged 103-mile-long barrier divided Berlin and symbolized the Cold War. When it began to crumble in 1989, so did the Soviet empire that had built it.

○ Hamlet's Castle, Elsinore, Denmark. Kronborg Castle, built 1577-1585, is the locale of Shakespeare's immortal tragedy "Hamlet."

Taj Mahal, Agra, India. One of the world's most beautiful buildings, erected 1631-1645 as a tomb for Mumtaz Mahal, wife of the Mogul emperor, Shah Jehan.

Chillon Castle, Vaud, Switzerland. This is the medieval castle at the eastern end of Lake Geneva in which Francois de Bonnivard, the Swiss hero commemorated by Lord Byron in his "Prisoner of Chillon," was imprisoned, 1530-1536.

Massachusetts Hall, Harvard University, Cambridge, Massachusetts. One of the oldest buildings on the campus, constructed in 1740.

Westminster Abbey, London, England. Several churches have stood on this historic site, the first built early in the 7th Century. The present structure goes back to 1245 when Henry III ordered the reconstruction of its predecessor. All English monarchs since William I have been crowned in Westminster.

Edinburgh Castle, Edinburgh, Scotland. Situated on a steep ridge, this historic castle overlooks the capital of Scotland. Of existing buildings that make up the castle group, St. Margaret's Chapel, built about 1100, is the oldest.

Stone Cannonball, Pevensey Castle, England. This castle was built in the 13th Century within the walls of the old Roman fortified town of Anderida. It is in the Sussex village of Pevensey, where William the Conqueror landed in 1066.

Wawel Castle, Krakow, Poland. Standing on Wawel Hill, the royal castle of the Polish monarchy was rebuilt in Italian Renaissance style in the 16th Century during the reign of Sigismund II.

Royal Castle, Stockholm, Sweden. Built at the beginning of the 18th Century from designs prepared by the famous Swedish architect Nicodemus Tessin.

Cathedral, Cologne, Germany (two stones). The stones represent this world-famous Gothic cathedral, construction of which began in 1248. The older is from the oldest part of the structure and came originally from the Rock of the Dragon quarries on the Rhine.

Fort San Antonio Abad, Manila, Philippines. Overlooking Manila Bay, this fort was a target of the mock bombardment agreed to by Adm. George Dewey during the Spanish-American War to gratify the traditional Spanish sense of honor and to save lives on both sides.

Parthenon, Athens, Greece. A temple sacred to the goddess Athena, built between 447 and 432 B.C., during the rule of Pericles.

Santa Lucia Barracks, Manila, Philippines. Part of an old Chinese gravestone, brought as ballast by Spanish ships at the beginning of the 17th Century, was used in the construction of Santa Lucia Barracks.

The Citadel, Jerusalem, Israel. Since the Middle Ages mistakenly known as "David's Castle" and "David's Tower."

Fort Santiago, Manila. Where the Philippine patriot Jose Rizal was executed by the Spanish in 1896.

Notre Dame Cathedral, Paris, France. The cornerstone of this historic church, regarded as the finest achievement of early Gothic architecture in France, was laid in 1163 and the building finished about 1230.

○ Ancient Temple, Hunan Province, China. The stone guardian angel found in the ruins of this temple is believed to have been carved in 564.

○ Old General Post Office, Dublin, Ireland. This building was held by Irish Republican troops under the leadership of Padraic Pearse during the Insurrection of Easter Week, 1916. From it, Pearse read the declaration of Ireland's independence.

MICHIGAN AVENUE - NATHAN HALE COURT

Temple, Forbidden City, Beijing, China (two stones). The roof of this early 15th Century pagoda was made of green tiles. Green was a royal color, second in standing only to yellow.

Winter Palace, Forbidden City, Beijing, China. The fragment is a yellow tile, representing the imperial color. Yellow tiles could be used only for covering imperial buildings. The Winter Palace was erected in the first quarter of the 15th Century.

Santa Sophia, Istanbul, Turkey. Regarded as the supreme glory of Byzantine architecture, this world-famous edifice was built from 532 to 562, during the reign of the Emperor Justinian. With the conquest by the Turks in 1453 of Constantinople (now Istanbul), the Christian Church of Santa Sophia (Holy Wisdom) became a mosque. In 1934 it was converted to a museum.

Arch of Triumph, Paris, France. This arch, one of the architectural glories of the French capital, was built on the decree of Napoleon I, whose victories it commemorates. In 1920 it became the burial place of France's Unknown Soldier.

Roof tile, Roman ruins, Birecik, Turkey. This relic is from a villa in Zeugma, a 2,000-year-old Roman garrison on the banks of the Euphrates River. The area is now an archeological site on the outskirts of Birecik, a modern city in southeastern Turkey.

United States Memorial, Mont Sec, France. Eight miles from the battlefield of St. Mihiel, where American troops won a decisive victory on Sept. 16, 1918, a Greek-style temple stands on Mont Sec as a memorial to the Americans who fell in this great battle.

Tower of Tears, Amsterdam, The Netherlands. This famous tower was built 10 years before Columbus first sailed to America. Standing by this tower, weeping wives and sweethearts bade sorrowful farewells to sailors leaving on voyages of exploration during the 15th and 16th Centuries. Henry Hudson sailed from this port for the New World in 1609.

Flodden Field, Northumberland, England. Here, on Sept. 9, 1513, the English under Thomas Howard, later third Duke of Norfolk, defeated the Scots under James IV, who was killed in the battle.

Viking Stone, Lake Malar Region, Sweden. This 170-pound Viking stone is an excellent example of the simple monuments that inhabitants of Sweden's Stone Age placed on the graves of their heroes.

Clementine Hall, Pontifical Palace, Vatican City, Italy. This is the residence of the popes.

Christ Church, Philadelphia, Pennsylvania. Completed in 1754, the church is considered one of the finest examples of Georgian architecture in the United States. Its pews once were occupied by Benjamin Franklin, George Washington and other noted Revolutionary War figures.

ANCIENT TEMPLE
HUNAN PROVINCE, CHINA

OLD GENERAL POST OFFICE
DUBLIN, IRELAND

ABRAHAM LINCOLN'S HOME
SPRINGFIELD, ILLINOIS

WORLD'S COLUMBIAN EXPOSITION
CHICAGO

BIRTHPLACE OF
COL. ROBERT R. McCORMICK

THE HOLY DOOR, ST. PETER'S
VATICAN CITY, ITALY

Powder Tower, Riga, Latvia. Built more than 700 years ago, this tower was part of the old fortifications of this ancient city on the Baltic Sea.

○ Abraham Lincoln's Home, Springfield, Illinois. The only home Lincoln ever owned was the five-year-old house he bought in 1844 and in which he lived until his departure for Washington as president in 1861. In this house, three of his four sons were born. Edward, his second son, died there.

Beaumaris Castle, Wales. King Edward I of England built this castle in 1295 to keep the Welsh in subjection. Here, one year later, Edward invited the bards of North Wales to a great banquet and, as they were about to eat, had them put to death.

Union Stock Yards Gate, Chicago. Erected about 1875 at 850 W. Exchange Ave., the three-part limestone gate formed the portal to Chicago's stockyards, where countless cattle, hogs and sheep were slaughtered. But the gate outlived the stockyards, which closed in 1971.

Fort Sumter, Charleston, South Carolina. Where the Civil War began following an attack by the Confederates, April 12-13, 1861.

Tainitzkaya Tower, the Kremlin, Moscow, Russia. Until Peter the Great removed the imperial court from Moscow to St. Petersburg in 1712, the Kremlin was headquarters of the Russian czars and of the patriarchs of the Russian Orthodox Church. Tainitzkaya Tower was built in 1498 and pulled down in 1933 because it interfered with traffic.

Bunker Hill Battlefield, Charlestown, Massachusetts. Where one of the most significant battles of the Revolutionary War was fought on June 17, 1775.

○ World's Columbian Exposition, Chicago. This famous World's Fair in 1893 commemorated the 400th anniversary of Columbus' landing in the New World.

Fort Marion, St. Augustine, Florida. Begun by the Spaniards in 1672 and completed approximately a century later, this fort was originally called Castle San Marcos. It was renamed in honor of the Revolutionary War hero Francis Marion when it came into possession of the United States.

○ Birthplace of Col. Robert R. McCormick. The Chicago Tribune's longtime editor and publisher was born on July 30, 1880, in a three-story house at 150 E. Ontario St., just east of the present North Michigan Avenue.

Douglas Hall, first University of Chicago. The first University of Chicago, immediate predecessor of the present institution, originated in a grant of land made by Stephen A. Douglas, who ran against Lincoln in the presidential campaign of 1860. It lasted from 1857 to 1886.

Mount McKinley, Denali National Park, Alaska. A chip off Mount McKinley, the highest peak in North America, made Alaska the last state to have a stone placed in Tribune Tower.

St. John's Episcopal Church, Richmond, Virginia. Here, on March 23, 1775, Patrick Henry made the historic address that concluded with the words, "Give me liberty or give me death."

The White House, Washington, D.C. This stone, from an inner wall of the White House, was obtained during the extensive alterations made in the executive mansion from 1950 to 1951.

Kensington Rune Stone, Kensington, Minnesota. This stone is from a spot close to where the famous Kensington rune stone was found in 1898. Engraved on the stone is an inscription indicating that Minnesota had been visited by a band of Norsemen ("8 Goths and 22 Norwegians") as early as 1362.

MICHIGAN AVENUE - NORTH WING

The Colosseum, Rome, Italy. Begun by the Emperor Vespasian in A.D. 72 and finished eight years later by Titus, his successor, this amphitheater, capable of accommodating 50,000 spectators, was the scene of gladiatorial combats and spectacles in which Christians were thrown to lions and other animals.

Stabian Baths, Pompeii, Italy. Buried with Herculaneum by an eruption of Mount Vesuvius in A.D. 79, Pompeii was a flourishing seaport and resort where many wealthy people lived in elaborate villas.

Badlands, South Dakota. Countless ages ago the famed Badlands region in the southwestern part of the state was covered by a vast salt sea. Covering approximately one million acres, they offer some of the world's most striking scenery.

○ The Holy Door, St. Peter's, Vatican City, Italy. Of the various doors leading into the interior of St. Peter's, the most famous is the Porta Santa or Holy Door, which is opened only in jubilee years—once every 25 years.

Monastery of St. Michael, Kiev, Ukraine. This golden-domed monastery, first built in 1108, is one of the great monuments of Ukrainian culture. Destroyed and rebuilt over the centuries, its latest renovation was carried out in the 1990s.

Great Wall of China, Shan-hai-kuan, Linyu, China. This brick is from the oldest part of the Great Wall—its juncture with the walls of Shan-hai-kuan, the ancient Chinese city now called Linyu.

Banteay Srei Hindu Temple, Angkor, Cambodia. Built around 967 of pink sandstone, it is the most intricately carved of all the temples in one of the world's great archeological sites, the Angkor complex. Its name means the "Citadel of the Women."

Ta Prohm Temple, Angkor, Cambodia. A ruin left intentionally unrestored, it remains in the same condition as when it was rediscovered by 19th Century French archeologists.

○ Great Pyramid of Cheops, Giza, Egypt. One of the original "Seven Wonders of the World," the Great Pyramid was built in the 30th Century B.C. It is the largest structure of its kind ever built, a solid mass of limestone 482 feet high and covering 13 acres.

○ Houses of Parliament, London, England. Built between 1840 and 1860, this great Gothic building is the assembly place of the House of Lords and the House of Commons. The ornamental stone head was removed from the eastern facade overlooking the River Thames.

Dome of St. Peter's, Vatican City, Italy. Largest and most widely known of all the churches of Christendom, St. Peter's took 181 years to build (1445-1626). Its majestic dome was completed, 1573-90, from designs left by Michelangelo, who died in 1564.

ILLINOIS STREET

Fort Ticonderoga, New York. Built by the French in 1755-56, Ticonderoga came into British possession when abandoned by the French in 1759. Shortly after the start of the American Revolution, it was captured without a shot by a small group of Americans led by Ethan Allen. Later reoccupied by the British, it was allowed to fall into ruins after the War of Independence. Reconstruction began in 1909.

William Henry Harrison Home, Vincennes, Indiana. The ninth president of the United States, Harrison was also the first governor of the Indiana Territory, created in 1800. His Vincennes home, built in 1803, contains 26 rooms and 13 fireplaces.

Mark Twain Cave, Hannibal, Missouri. This stone was taken from a spot in the cave near where, according to Twain's classic "Tom Sawyer," Injun Joe buried the treasure later discovered by Tom and Huckleberry Finn.

Rotunda, Mammoth Cave, Kentucky. One of the world's greatest natural wonders, Mammoth Cave has five levels covering an area 10 miles in circumference. The Rotunda is a huge natural hall where visitors can still see the saltpeter vats used in the War of 1812.

○ Independence Hall, Philadelphia, Pennsylvania. Many regard this as the nation's most significant building, a shrine immortalized by such scenes as the appointment of George Washington as commander of the Continental Army, July 16, 1775; the signing of the Declaration of Independence, July 4, 1776; and the adoption of the Constitution of the United States, Sept. 17, 1787.

Walls of Derry, Londonderry, Northern Ireland. In 1689 Williamite forces holding this Irish town (known as Derry until 1608) successfully withstood a 105-day siege by the army of England's recently deposed James II.

Nassau Hall, Princeton University, Princeton, New Jersey. Princeton's first college building, completed in 1756, was named in honor of William III of England, formerly Prince of Nassau and of Orange. Cannon fire scarred its walls during the Battle of Princeton, Jan. 3, 1777, when Nassau Hall changed hands three times.

Chimney Rock, Nebraska. This natural landmark near Bayard in the western part of the state is a mound of reddish sandstone covering about 40 acres and surmounted by a slender shaft of rock approximately 150 feet high.

Little America, Antarctica. This site, on the Bay of Whales, Ross Sea, was used as the base of the Antarctic expeditions of 1928-30, 1933-35 and 1946-47, led by Adm. Richard Byrd.

International Peace Garden, North Dakota. This unique 2,200-acre tract crossing the U.S.-Canadian border commemorates the peaceful relations that have always existed between the two countries.

GREAT PYRAMID OF CHEOPS
GIZA, EGYPT

HOUSES OF PARLIAMENT
LONDON, ENGLAND

INDEPENDENCE HALL
PHILADELPHIA, PENNSYLVANIA

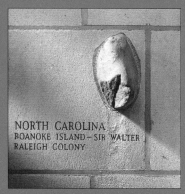

FORT RALEIGH
ROANOKE ISLAND, NORTH CAROLINA

CUSTER BATTLEFIELD
MONTANA

John Brown's Cabin, Osawatomie, Kansas. This stone is from the foundation of the cabin occupied by the militant abolitionist after he and his five grown sons had arrived in Kansas following their decision to leave Ohio.

Port Louisa, Iowa. It was in the vicinity of this town on the Mississippi that the first white men, a small group that included Pere Jacques Marquette and Louis Joliet, set foot on what is now Iowa soil, June 25, 1673.

Gaspee Point, Narragansett Bay, Rhode Island. Located on the Providence River arm of the bay, this is the point where a group of American patriots destroyed the Gaspee, a British armed schooner, on June 10, 1772.

Old Swedes Church, Wilmington, Delaware. Swedish settlers began arriving in Delaware as early as 1638. The church, now Holy Trinity, is one of the oldest in North America, built in 1698.

○ Fort Raleigh, Roanoke Island, North Carolina. Because of the still-unexplained disappearance in the late 16th Century of 116 men, women and children from Roanoke, this English settlement has come to be known as the "Lost Colony."

Nelson House, Yorktown, Virginia. Built shortly before 1740, this was the home of Gen. Thomas Nelson, who succeeded Thomas Jefferson as governor of Virginia. During the final days of the siege of Yorktown, the Nelson home was the headquarters of Lord Cornwallis.

Old Fur Trading Post, Prairie du Chien, Wisconsin. In 1835, 13 years before Wisconsin was admitted to the Union, Joseph Rolette, agent for John Jacob Astor's American Fur Company, built this two-story stone house.

Old Chapel, Yale University, New Haven, Connecticut. Successor to the university's first chapel, erected in 1763, Old Chapel was finished in 1824. Converted in 1876 into lecture rooms, it was razed in 1896.

Ancient Town Hall, Stockholm, Sweden. The medieval town hall was located on the main square of Stockholm's Old Town. Its gable faced the square's north side, while its first floor housed a large council chamber. The building was demolished in the 18th Century.

Fort William and Mary, New Castle, New Hampshire. As early as 1631 this site was fortified. Fort William and Mary, built 1704-05, was the scene of one of the first blows struck for American liberty when in mid-December 1774, the British garrison was compelled to surrender to a party of Americans led by Capt. John Pickering and Maj. John Langdon.

Sibyl's Cave, Cumae, Naples, Italy. Cumae, built in the 9th or 8th Century B.C., was regarded as the earliest Greek colony in Italy. The cave is where the Cumaean Sibyl, the priestess of Apollo mentioned by Virgil, uttered her prophecies.

John Brown's Fort, Harpers Ferry, West Virginia. When on the night of Oct. 16, 1859, John Brown's raid on the armory in Harpers Ferry went awry, he and 21 followers took refuge in the armory engine house, ever since known as "John Brown's Fort."

Chimney Point, Lake Champlain, Vermont. Standing on this site on July 30, 1609, Samuel de Champlain, first governor of French Canada, gave his name to the lake which it overlooked. The lake was the scene, 200 years later, of Commodore Thomas MacDonough's impressive victory over a British naval force.

Confederate Prison, Andersonville, Georgia. Established by the Confederate states in November 1863, this military prison was in use from March 1864 to April 1865. During those 13 months, 49,495 Union troops were held there, as many as 33,006 at one time. More than 13,000 prisoners died within its confines.

○ Custer Battlefield, Montana. On June 25, 1876, Gen. George A. Custer and his command, consisting of 231 officers, enlisted men, civilians and Indian scouts, were wiped out here in a battle with an overwhelming force of Indians.

Fort McHenry, Baltimore, Maryland. Here, during a 25-hour bombardment by a British fleet, Francis Scott Key was inspired to write "The Star-Spangled Banner." The fort was named in honor of James McHenry, secretary of war from 1786 to 1800.

Battlefield, New Orleans, Louisiana. The brick shown is from the ruins of the De La Ronde home, known in 1815 as the Versailles Plantation. This house was located in the area occupied by Andrew Jackson before he moved his troops to a stronger line nearer New Orleans.

Cumberland Gap, Tennessee. Named in honor of William, Duke of Cumberland, victor of the Battle of Culloden in 1746, this historic mountain pass provided a natural highway for thousands of settlers, hunters and trappers heading for Kentucky and points west.

Petra, Jordan. This ancient stronghold of the Nabataeans was, up to the time of its inclusion in the Roman Empire, A.D. 106, the center of a great caravan trade. The ruins of this ancient rock city are located southeast of the Dead Sea and are enclosed on three sides by mountain walls of rose-colored sandstone.

Shirley House, Vicksburg, Mississippi.
Taken by Union troops during the 47-day siege by Gen. Ulysses Grant, this house was saved from destruction because of the urgent pleas of Mrs. James Shirley. She, her husband and 15-year-old son occupied the house, built in 1833.

Fort Brady, Sault Ste. Marie, Michigan.
The first military outpost on this historic site was erected by the French in 1751. The United States flag did not fly over the fort until 1820. A new fort was built in 1822 and named in honor of its first commander, Col. Hugh Brady.

Tawasa, near Montgomery, Alabama.
In the spring of 1540, Hernando de Soto, the Spanish soldier-explorer, is believed to have spent a week at the ancient Indian town of Tawasa.

○ Birthplace of Elijah Lovejoy, Albion, Maine. Ardent abolitionist and martyr in the cause of freedom of the press, Elijah Parish Lovejoy was born Nov. 9, 1802, about three miles from Albion. Because of the strong anti-slavery views expressed in his newspaper, the *Alton Observer,* a pro-slavery mob in that Illinois town attacked the warehouse in which he had stored a new printing press. They shot Lovejoy to death and destroyed the press.

Put-in-Bay, Lake Erie, Ohio. Scene of Commodore Oliver Hazard Perry's decisive victory over the British fleet, Sept. 10, 1813.

Ancient Gate, Walls of Suwon, South Korea.
One of the oldest cities in Korea, Suwon was captured by U.S. troops during the Korean War.

Site of De Soto's Landing, Arkansas.
Twenty miles south of Helena, Arkansas, is the spot at which Hernando De Soto first set foot on Arkansas soil during his historic voyage down the Mississippi.

Ludendorff Bridge, Remagen, Germany.
When the Allies advanced into Germany in 1945, this was the only bridge across the Rhine that had not been destroyed. Seized by Allied troops on March 8, the bridge collapsed March 17, 1945.

Town Hall, St. Lo, France. Administrative center of the ancient French town of St. Lo (pillaged by Norsemen in 889), this building was leveled by American artillery while preparing for the breakthrough in July 1944, which led to the liberation of France.

German Pillbox, Omaha Beach, France.
Wrecked by United States naval gunfire, this pillbox was one of the fortifications of the central Normandy beaches made famous by the landing of American troops during the invasion of France, June 6-10, 1944.

City Hall, Aachen, Germany. Situated on the German-Belgian border, Aachen (called Aix-la-Chapelle by the Belgians and French) was the second capital of Charlemagne's empire and was that ruler's favorite residence after 768. In World War II, it was heavily bombarded and almost destroyed by the Allied armies before its surrender on Oct. 20, 1944.

Tower Gate, Aachen, Germany. The stone is from one of the medieval tower gates built at various places in the walls of this richly historic city.

City Palace, Potsdam, Germany. During World War II, Allied bombs heavily damaged the palace, built in the 17th Century and once a residence for Prussian royalty. The Communist government of East Germany completed its destruction, but the parliament of the German state of Brandenburg plans to rebuild it as the legislature's new home.

Mt. Taptochau, Saipan, Northern Mariana Islands, Western Pacific. From this peak the Japanese directed severe artillery fire on American soldiers and marines during their conquest of the island in June 1944.

Bloody Nose Ridge, Peleliu, Palau, Western Pacific. This stone is from the rugged coral ridge north of Peleliu's vital airfield where Japanese troops were powerfully dug in during the bitter fighting from Sept. 14 to Oct. 13, 1944, which ended in the island's capture by the invading Americans. The First Marine Division suffered heavy casualties in establishing the beachhead.

Seminaire de Quebec, Quebec City, Canada. The seminary sent priests as far away as the Mississippi Valley and the Gulf of Mexico to set up missions. This limestone block comes from the seminary's administrative wing, built in 1678.

○ Pearl Harbor, Oahu, Hawaii. This stone is from the shore of the harbor, a few hundred yards from the site of the Japanese attack that came without warning on Dec. 7, 1941.

Kwajalein, Marshall Islands, Western Pacific. Strongly fortified by the Japanese, this coral atoll was captured by troops of the U.S. Seventh Division in the fighting from Jan. 30 to Feb. 6, 1944.

Orote Peninsula, Guam. Forming the south side of Apra Harbor, this is the site of the bloody battle in which the First Provisional Marine Brigade wrested control of the island's only usable airfield from the Japanese in July 1944.

○ Luxembourg Palace, Paris, France. Built between 1615 and 1630 for Marie de Medici, mother of Louis XIII, this famous Renaissance palace has been the scene of many outstanding

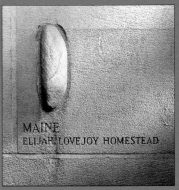

BIRTHPLACE OF ELIJAH LOVEJOY
ALBION, MAINE

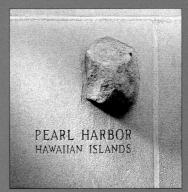

PEARL HARBOR
OAHU, HAWAII

LUXEMBOURG PALACE
PARIS, FRANCE

SANTA MARIA ISLAND, AZORES

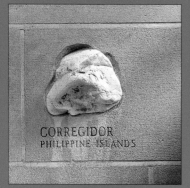

CORREGIDOR, PHILIPPINES

CLIFF DWELLING
MESA VERDE, COLORADO

events in history. Used as a prison during the French Revolution, it was where Napoleon was crowned Emperor of France in 1804.

Anzio Beach, Italy. Thirty-three miles southeast of Rome, this ancient port was the site of the amphibious landing by U.S. and British troops, Jan. 22, 1944. Here, on March 25, after severe fighting, the Allied drive on Rome began.

Petrified Forest, Calistoga, California. Approximately five million years ago in what is now Napa County, a mighty volcanic eruption showered lava on a forest of giant redwood trees and turned them to stone.

House of Commons, London, England. Covering eight acres, the Houses of Parliament are the meeting place of England's top legislative bodies, the House of Commons and the House of Lords. The House of Commons was badly damaged by German air raids on May 10, 1941.

Fort Clatsop, near Astoria, Oregon. Site of the blockhouse and stockade erected by the historic Lewis and Clark expedition. Here Captains Meriwether Lewis and William Clark (a younger brother of George Rogers Clark) and their band of pioneers spent the winter of 1805.

Mosaic Hall, Reichschancellery, Berlin, Germany. Before World War II, this was the office of the Chancellor, chief minister of state in Germany. The building was severely damaged by Allied planes in World War II.

Toyotomi Castle, Osaka, Japan. Originally known as the "Golden Castle," this unique structure was begun by the Emperor Hideyoshi in 1583 and finished two years later. Some 50,000 men were engaged in its construction.

Mount Rainier, Washington. This majestic peak, 14,408 feet high, was discovered in 1792 by the English navigator, Capt. George Vancouver, who named it for Adm. Peter Rainier of the British Navy. In 1899 the area around the mountain, covering 324 square miles, was designated a national park.

○ Santa Maria Island, Azores. Columbus landed here on Feb. 18, 1493, on his way to Spain as he returned from his first voyage to the New World.

○ Corregidor, Philippines. After the Japanese invasion of the Philippines in December 1941, this island in Manila Bay was selected as a leading defense position by Gen. Douglas MacArthur. After heroic resistance, it surrendered on May 6, 1942. It was retaken by returning American troops in February 1945.

Old Washoe County Courthouse, Reno, Nevada. Reno, named for Gen. Jesse L. Reno, a Union officer killed at the Battle of Stone Mountain, became the county seat in 1871. The courthouse was begun two years later.

Hans Christian Andersen Home, Odense, Denmark. Born in 1805, the beloved writer of fairy tales left Odense when he was 14 to seek his fortune in Copenhagen. Andersen created "The Ugly Duckling," "The Brave Tin Soldier" and many other immortal tales.

Mormon Temple, Salt Lake City, Utah. The first cornerstone of this magnificent temple of the Church of Jesus Christ of Latter-Day Saints was laid in 1853. The temple was dedicated 40 years later when construction was completed.

Craters of the Moon National Monument, Idaho. Unique among natural wonders of North America is this 47,000-acre lava field in south central Idaho. It offers an abundance of moonlike scenery.

Yellowstone National Park, Wyoming. Approximately 3,450 square miles in area, Yellowstone Park offers a treasury of scenic beauty. The stone is from Obsidian Cliff, a mountainside of volcanic glass, black and sparkling, from which Indians made their arrowheads.

Petrified Forest, Arizona. Situated near Holbrook, Navajo County, this extraordinary collection of petrified coniferous trees covers 85,000 acres and is estimated to be 150 million years old.

Aztec Ruins National Monument, New Mexico. The ruins from which this stone was taken are of a 450-room community building near the town of Aztec in northwestern New Mexico. This structure was built in the 12th Century by ancestral Pueblo Indians and not, as the name of the monument would seem to indicate, by the Aztecs of Mexico.

○ Cliff Dwelling, Mesa Verde, Colorado. The stone is from the ruins of one of the cliff dwellings built as long ago as the 12th or 13th Century by the ancestral Pueblo Indians.

Boston Avenue Methodist Church, Tulsa, Oklahoma. This beautiful church, completed in 1929, is an outstanding example of modern ecclesiastical architecture. On its lower floors are an auditorium, chapel, community hall, gymnasium, kitchen and educational rooms. The auditorium seats 2,000 and the community hall, 1,200.

Miraflores Locks, Panama Canal. Completed in 1913, the two-flight set of locks raises or lowers ships a total of 54 feet as they pass between the Pacific and Atlantic Oceans. This 60-pound concrete block is from the locks on the canal's Pacific Ocean entrance.

Medieval Sculpture
in a Modern Spirit

Although it may seem overwhelmingly serious, a monument with a capital "M," Tribune Tower actually is one of the most whimsical skyscrapers in Chicago. The reason: the strange sculptures that cover the top and bottom of the building. They are known, as their medieval predecessors were, as grotesques.

As early guidebooks to the Tower explain, these carvings were intended to wittily express the ideals of journalism, much like an editorial cartoon. Above the Tower's main entrance arch, for example, is a grotesque of a whispering man, his fingers conspiratorially pressed to his lips. This figure, according to a 1930s guidebook, symbolizes insidious rumor. Alongside it is a flaming head of a shouting man. It personifies news (and, one supposes, a very hot story).

More journalism-related grotesques are tucked beneath the Tower's fourth-floor windows, an appropriate place because the fourth floor houses the *Chicago Tribune's* newsroom. As in medieval cathedrals, these grotesques are part of an architectural feature called a corbel—in this case, a block of stone projecting diagonally from the wall.

One of the grotesques, a wise old owl clutching a camera, represents observation and caution. Nearby are a frog, suggesting those who are ever-

MODERN MORALITY PLAY
Bringing medieval art into the modern age, many of the sculptures that adorn the walls of Tribune Tower teach humorous lessons about the profession of journalism. This pair, a whispering man and a shouting man, symbolizes the difference between rumor and news.

SAD SPINES
The porcupine, with a horn in his paws, symbolizes intolerance and arrogance.

LACK OF FORESIGHT
The cat, holding a beggar's tin cup, represents the sad outcome of improvidence.

HARDLY ROYAL
The crowned dog, his paw caught in a mousetrap, stands for pomposity.

RASCAL RODENT
The rat, bearing a musket, characterizes cruelty and maliciousness.

BELOW THE FOURTH-FLOOR WINDOWS

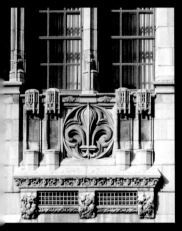

UNDYING GLORY
The Tower's many fleurs-de-lis honor American valor on the battlefields of France during World War I. Three grotesques are located below this fleur-de-lis.

GALLERY OF GROTESQUES
The frog (clockwise, from top left) suggests those who are ever alert and eager to be heard. Holding his nose and wearing spectacles, the elephant evokes scandal. The ape is an example of the familiar busybody. Clutching a camera, the wise old owl personifies observation and caution.

alert, and an ape, exemplifying the familiar busybody. A spectacled, nose-holding elephant typifies scandal. Could there be a better symbol for Chicago, where it seems another alderman goes to prison every month?

Tribune Tower doesn't have any gargoyles, those long, protruding carvings of mythical monsters that channeled rainwater away from Europe's great cathedrals. But both gargoyles and grotesques allowed medieval stone masons to deliver biting social commentaries, exposing the foibles of greedy monks, cowardly knights and usurious merchants. In the same spirit, the Tower's architects targeted certain types of people in modern life.

Above the fourth-floor windows, amid the filigree of the Gothic ornament, is a porcupine with a horn in its paws; it is supposed to symbolize intolerance and arrogance. Close by is a cat holding a beggar's tin cup, representing the sad consequences of neglecting future needs. A crowned dog, his paw caught in a mousetrap, stands for pomposity. A monkey, with a cap and bauble, is a symbol of folly. And a rat, bearing an old-fashioned musket, suggests cruelty and maliciousness.

To emphasize that they were not trying to re-create a medieval cathedral, but to design a modern variation of it, Tribune Tower architects John Mead Howells and Raymond M. Hood used carvings of American plant, animal and insect life as border decorations for the grotesques. The grotesques below the fourth-floor windows, for example, are surrounded with carvings representing the American plane tree and the pine leaf.

The grotesques are not limited to the Tower's lower reaches. On the former 25th-floor observatory, likenesses of bats are carved into the underside of the Tower's flying buttresses. They are its equivalent of the bats in the belfry. (The Tower's summit does have a set of chimes that once rang on the quarter-hour, but they are no longer used.)

Who designed the grotesques and determined where they went? Architectural historians and present-day sculptors believe that Howells and Hood did concept drawings for the grotesques, then hired sculptors to make clay models. A stone carver would have executed the designs, working with chisels, wooden mallets and small, hand-held pneumatic hammers. The grotesques were anchored in place by a variety of means, including steel pins.

Today, in the opinion of those who prefer sleek modern buildings, such decoration is fruitless because few passersby can understand it—and even fewer can see it on upper floors. But there's another view: Ornament such as the Tower's grotesques provides big, imposing buildings with much-needed doses of humor and human scale.

Even better, the grotesques allow architecture to tell a story—here, a narrative of human virtues and vices. Nothing could be more fitting, given that a newspaper is a daily chronicle of what we do, both the good and (all too often) the bad.

ANIMAL ART
Below the fourth-floor windows, the ape and the bear are representatives of activism and its opposite, indolence.

BATS IN THE BELFRY
The playful spirit of the lower-level grotesques continues in the former outdoor observatory on the 25th floor of Tribune Tower.

CHAPTER FOUR

Storytelling in Stone

Tribune Tower's arched entrance shelters a monumental stone screen, called Aesop's Screen because it showcases carved stone characters from Aesop's fables.

These weird figures, age-old symbols of human virtues and vices, perch among the branches of a delicately carved tree. Also present are whimsical carvings symbolizing the *Tribune's* former editors and Tribune Tower's architects. The figures, which are visible from either side of the entrance, are not easy to identify. But with help from the accompanying chart, visitors should be able to make them out.

Because the Aesop's characters are visible from within the Tower's main lobby, where quotations celebrating the freedom of the press are chiseled into the walls, they present a sharp contrast between different kinds of storytelling. To the writer of fiction and fable, imagination and distortion are essential elements to entertain and delight the reader. But to the reporter—whether on a newspaper, a television or radio station, or the Internet—ferreting out the facts remains the essence of journalism.

An explanation of the characters in Aesop's Screen, and their imagery, follows.

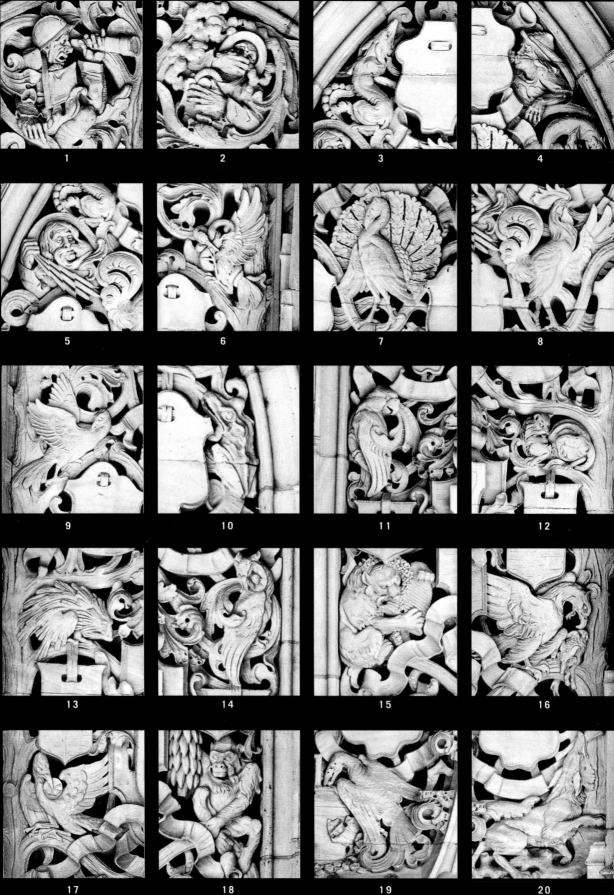

AN EXPLANATION OF THE CHARACTERS IN AESOP'S SCREEN

1, 2 Tribune editors and publishers. Figures commemorating the *Chicago Tribune's* co-editors and co-publishers, Col. Robert R. McCormick and Capt. Joseph M. Patterson, in World War I.

3,4 The Howling Dog and Robin Hood. Humorous characterizations of John Mead Howells and Raymond M. Hood, architects of Tribune Tower.

5 Zeus. Mythical ruler of gods and men, whose most effective weapons were thunderbolts—and whose favorite bird was the eagle.

6 The Raven and the Serpent. A hungry raven decided to eat a snake, which he had discovered lying asleep. On being seized in the bird's beak, however, the snake bit the raven with his poisonous fangs. "I am justly served," gasped the dying raven, "for trying to profit by injuring others."

7 The Peacock and the Crane. A peacock, strutting around, spread his gorgeous tail and, boasting of his beauty, ridiculed the somber colors of the crane. "Tell me," said the crane, "is it better to strut about in the mud as you do, or to soar above the clouds as I do?"

8,9 The Partridge and the Cocks. A partridge was captured by a man, who clipped his wings and put him in a pen with some gamecocks. The cocks were not civil to the partridge, who thought they were cruel because he was a stranger. Later, he saw them fighting each other and understood why they acted as they did.

10 The Frog. Remembering the humorous nickname given the French by American soldiers in World War I, a frog has been carved into the screen, to represent J.A. Fouilhoux, an associate of Howells and Hood, architects of Tribune Tower.

11 The Parrot. A warning against idle talk, senseless repetition and servile imitation.

12 The Cat and the Fox. A fox, who boasted a hundred ways of escaping his enemies, was caught by the hounds, while the cat, who preferred one safe way, sat unharmed in the tree.

13 The Porcupine and the Snakes. A porcupine begged to be sheltered in the cave of some snakes, who readily admitted him. His sharp quills so annoyed them, however, that they soon regretted their unthinking hospitality and asked him to leave. "I am quite satisfied where I am," said the porcupine, "but you may leave, if you wish."

14 The Owl. Symbol of wisdom.

15 The Bear and the Beehive. A bear, searching for honey, attacked a beehive and was promptly stung. He who wantonly hurts others places himself in a position to be hurt by others.

16 The Eagle and the Fox. One day an eagle carried off the cub of his good friend and neighbor, the fox. On discovering his loss, the fox scolded the eagle and begged him to return his loved one. The eagle, thinking himself secure up in the tree, refused. Then the fox built a fire under the tree and the eagle, fearing for the safety of his own offspring, returned the cub to the fox.

17 The Fox and the Crow. A hungry crow, enjoying a piece of cheese on a tree branch, was flattered by a wily fox into singing a song. At the first note, however, the cheese fell to the ground and was promptly devoured by the fox.

18 The Wolf, the Fox and the Ape. A wolf accused a fox of stealing, but the fox denied the charge. The case was tried before an ape, who after hearing all the evidence said: "I do not think you, Wolf, ever lost what you claim; and I do believe you, Fox, to have stolen what you so stoutly deny."

19 The Crow and the Pitcher. A crow, whose throat was parched from thirst, came upon a pitcher with a little water in the bottom. He tried desperately to reach the water, but, failing each time, was about to give up in despair when an idea occurred to him. Slowly, one by one, he dropped pebbles into the pitcher, until they forced the water up to where he could drink.

20 The Fox and the Grapes. A fox, stealing into a vineyard, noticed a particularly luscious bunch of grapes hanging from the top of a vine. He climbed and jumped after them time after time without success until at last, giving up in disgust, he exclaimed, "I don't want those grapes anyway—I'm sure they were sour."

21 The Boar and the Fox. A fox chanced one day upon a boar carefully sharpening his tusks against a tree. "Why," he asked, "do you prepare for battle when there are no enemies in sight?" "Because," replied the boar, "when enemies are in sight, I may not have time to sharpen my tusks."

22 The Wolf and the Crane. A wolf, in whose throat a bone had stuck, promised anything to him who would remove it. A crane offered to help and at last succeeded in dislodging the bone. But when he claimed his reward, the wolf replied with a growl, "Be content—you have put your head into a wolf's mouth and taken it out again. That is enough reward."

21

22

To the writer of fiction and fable, imagination and distortion are essential elements to entertain and delight the reader. But to the reporter, ferreting out the facts remains the essence of journalism.

Shrine to a Free Press

n a cathedral of commerce like Tribune Tower, it should come as no surprise that the main lobby resembles the nave of a church. So thoroughly is this room imbued with an ecclesiastical spirit that a visitor might reasonably expect to encounter a clergyman at the ornate oak desk. Yet the lobby is hardly Notre Dame-on-the-prairie. Like the rest of the Tower, it has quirks and faults.

Known as the Hall of Inscriptions, the lobby was conceived as a secular shrine that celebrates the ideals and obligations of a free press. Chiseled into its travertine marble walls are quotations such as the 1st Amendment to the Constitution, visible on the wall opposite the guard desk. There are many others, including these words from James Madison: "To the press alone, checkered as it is with abuses, the world is indebted for all the triumphs which have been gained by reason and humanity over error and oppression."

Dominating the room is a large relief map that depicts North America and a tiny portion of South America. Initially, much more of South America was shown, but the *Tribune's* ardently patriotic editor and publisher, Col. Robert R. McCormick, apparently wanted North America (and thus the United States) to be more prominent. So the lower two feet of the map—and vast swaths of Colombia, Ecuador and Peru—were unceremoniously chopped off.

Said to be the largest relief map of the United States when it was installed in 1927, the display is made of plaster mixed with retired U.S. currency; the exceptionally tough paper on which money is printed offered greater durability than if plaster alone had been used. In keeping with the religious theme of the lobby, the map is framed by a decorative oak screen typically found behind a church altar and known as a reredos (pronounced RARE-ah-dahs).

DETAIL

A SLIP OF THE CHISEL

The art of stone carving is as subject to human error as any other endeavor, as one of the inscriptions in Tribune Tower's main lobby makes clear. Note the "S" that had to be inserted in the quote from Chief Justice Charles Evans Hughes after a carver left out that letter. The inscription is on the west wall to the left of Aesop's Screen.

Churchlike elements can be found throughout the room, from the eight arched window insets on the north and south walls to the carved stone screen above the entrance. Recalling the depictions of saints often found over the doors of medieval cathedrals, the screen shows characters from Aesop's fables, each representing a moral. Four bronze chandeliers cast a soft glow and give the room an appropriate aura of dignity. The ceiling beams, which resemble dark wood but actually are painted plaster, contribute to the restrained tone.

While the Hall of Inscriptions faithfully continues the neo-Gothic style of the Tower's exterior, subtle differences endow it with its own character. In contrast to the cool, gray Indiana limestone that clads the skyscraper, the lobby's travertine walls are warm in feel and creamy in color, almost buttery. The overall effect is at once welcoming and awe-inspiring, a rare combination of power and serenity.

Inlaid in the lobby floor is a quotation from the 19th Century English critic John Ruskin that articulates the aesthetic ideals that inspired the Tower's creators. "Let us think as we lay stone on stone," it says, "that a time is to come when those stones will be held sacred."

Yet few works of architecture, especially the lobbies of big-city office buildings, are either perfect or fixed in time; the Hall of Inscriptions certainly has proved no exception, largely because it is flanked by shops and offices whose functions are far from spiritual. During the 1960s, when ground-floor space just off the Hall of Inscriptions was occupied by a Kohler Company showroom, the rectangular, eye-level windows in the stately lobby showcased toilets and other bathroom fixtures. Decades earlier, offices behind the upper-level, arched windows contributed visual clutter with their desks and filing cabinets. In the 1940s, these windows were filled with limestone.

The shifting winds of architectural fashion also have altered the lobby's look. The original, ornate guard desk was removed in the 1930s when the sleek forms of Art Deco would have made it look outdated. The first version of the reredos didn't last much longer; it is thought to have been eliminated around 1939 after the *Tribune* donated the relief map to Chicago's Field Museum of Natural History. Over the years, the map space was filled with a huge American flag, patriotic murals and finally, reflecting the rise of modern architecture, a tall, gray marble slab that gave visitors a chilly welcome.

The slab came down in 1990, when the lobby was handsomely restored by Chicago architects Vinci/Hamp. Relying on old photographs and blueprints, they designed replicas of the initial reredos and guard desk. As part of the project, the relief map, which had been used as a geology exhibit at the Field Museum, was reinstalled. Meanwhile, limestone was removed from the windows on the north and south walls and the reopened windows were lit with artificial light and adorned with drapes.

So successful was the restoration that it spawned imitators within Tribune Tower. The first occurred in 1997, the *Chicago Tribune's* 150th anniversary of publishing, in the Nathan Hale Lobby, a modestly scaled room found to the north of the Hall of Inscriptions. Once designed in a style that charitably could be called Early Space Age Modern, the Hale lobby was given a more formal look by Vinci/Hamp, with new travertine marble walls and its own set of inscriptions. At the same time, Vinci/Hamp renovated Harmony Hall, which connects the Hall of Inscriptions and Nathan Hale Lobby.

In 1998, the *Tribune's* fourth-floor reception area underwent a similar conversion in a project done in separate stages by the Austin Company of Des Plaines and Eva Maddox Associates of Chicago. The reception area's walls were covered in travertine and fitted with bronze plaques commemorating the *Tribune's* Pulitzer Prize winners. In another echo of the Hall of Inscriptions, the First Amendment was inscribed in a wall of travertine.

Behind the Hall of Inscriptions are elevator lobbies where the walls are chiseled with additional quotations about freedom of the press. Under the arches leading to the elevators are plaques honoring *Chicago Tribune* employees who served in the First and Second World Wars. The carved supports of the oak archway beams symbolize the progress created by technological advances in wind, water, steam and electricity. One of the elevators, at the far end of the north elevator lobby, used to be a private car for McCormick, which whisked him to his palatial quarters on the 24th floor.

DROP DEAD DELICACY
The doors of the Tribune Tower elevators feature whimsical Gothic metalwork that is comparable in spirit to the building's grotesques.

HISTORY ON PARADE
Historic front pages from the *Chicago Tribune* are displayed in a hallway off the Nathan Hale Lobby. They are engraved in copper and surrounded in a bronze frame.

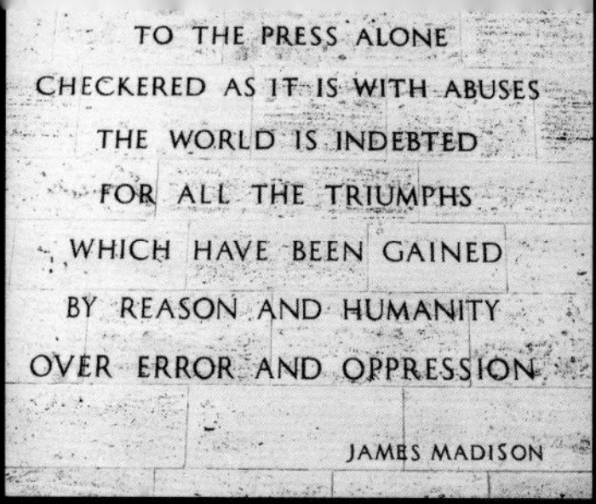

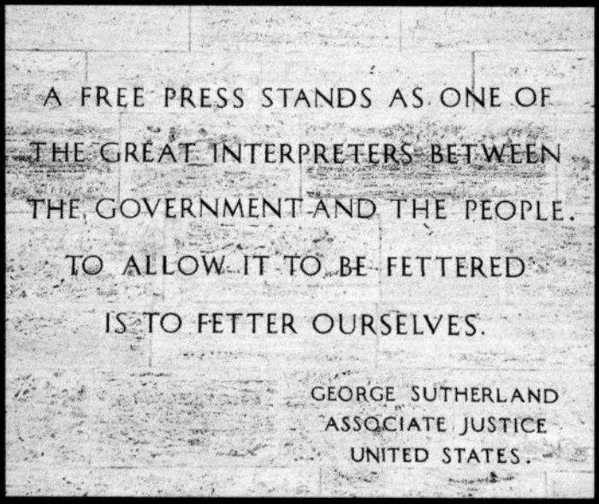

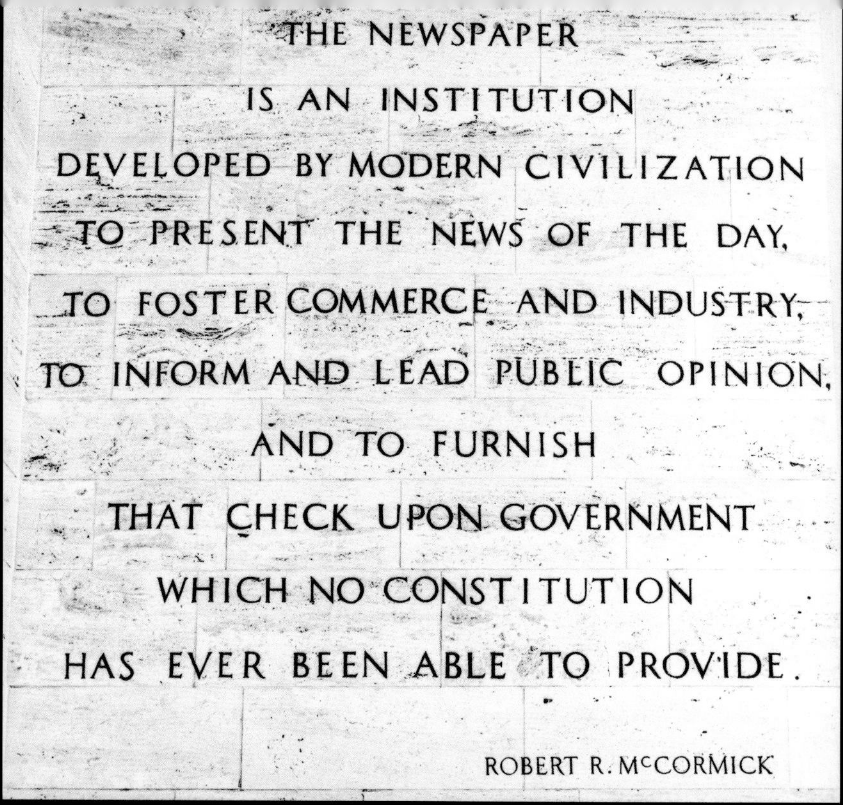

THE NEWSPAPER
IS AN INSTITUTION
DEVELOPED BY MODERN CIVILIZATION
TO PRESENT THE NEWS OF THE DAY,
TO FOSTER COMMERCE AND INDUSTRY,
TO INFORM AND LEAD PUBLIC OPINION,
AND TO FURNISH
THAT CHECK UPON GOVERNMENT
WHICH NO CONSTITUTION
HAS EVER BEEN ABLE TO PROVIDE.

ROBERT R. McCORMICK

"The mass of every people must be barbarous where there is no printing, and consequently knowledge is not generally diffused. Knowledge is diffused among our people by newspapers."

—*Samuel Johnson*

A GUIDE TO THE INSCRIPTIONS AND THEIR LOCATIONS

Few products are as perishable as newspapers, but in Tribune Tower's main lobby, known as the Hall of Inscriptions, newspapers—or, more precisely, powerful statements about them—become as permanent as stone. Carved into the lobby's walls of travertine marble during the early and middle years of the 20th Century, these quotations give monumental expression to the ideal of freedom of the press. They also celebrate liberty, truth and courage in battle, all values held dear by longtime *Tribune* editor and publisher Robert R. McCormick. He is thought to have made the final decision on which quotations appeared in the Hall of Inscriptions. Not surprisingly, given the way McCormick put his personal stamp on Tribune Tower, he is the source of three of the 27 quotations that appear in the Hall of Inscriptions and its adjoining elevator lobbies. The others come from a range of distinguished figures, from American presidents to French philosophers.

Inscribing stone walls with quotations is a living tradition at Tribune Tower. To mark the *Chicago Tribune's* 150th anniversary of publishing on June 10, 1997, six quotations were chiseled into the travertine marble walls of the renovated Nathan Hale Lobby, which is just north of the Hall of Inscriptions. The quotations were culled from more than 600 suggestions submitted by readers and *Tribune* employees.

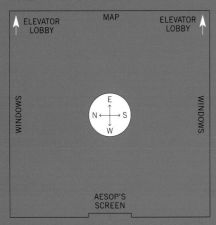

MAP

ELEVATOR LOBBY

ELEVATOR LOBBY

WINDOWS

WINDOWS

N E S W

AESOP'S SCREEN

WEST WALL (LEFT OF AESOP'S SCREEN)

"Congress shall make no law respecting an establishment of religion or prohibiting the free exercise thereof, or abridging the freedom of speech or of the press, or the right of the people peaceably to assemble and to petition the government for a redress of grievances."
—*The First Amendment to the Constitution, 1791.*

"The administration of government has become more complex. The opportunities for malfeasance and corruption have multiplied. Crime has grown to most serious proportions. And the danger of its protection by unfaithful officials and of the impairment of the fundamental security of life and property by criminal alliances and official neglect, emphasize the primary need of a vigilant and courageous press especially in great cities. The fact that the liberty of the press may be abused by miscreant purveyors of scandal does not make any the less necessary the immunity of the press from previous restraint in dealing with official misconduct."
—*Chief Justice Charles Evans Hughes, from a decision of the U.S. Supreme Court, June 1, 1931.*

WEST WALL (RIGHT OF AESOP'S SCREEN)

"This is true liberty, when free-born men having to advise the public, may speak free which he who can, and will, deserves high praise, who neither can, nor will, may hold his peace: What can be juster in a state than this?"
—*The Greek tragedian Euripides, from "The Suppliant Women," a patriotic play written in 421 B.C.*

"Give me but the liberty of the press and I will give to the minister a venal House of Peers. I will give him a corrupt and servile House of Commons. I will give him the full swing of the patronage of office. I will give him the whole host of ministerial influence. I will give him all the power that place can confer upon him to purchase up submission and overawe resistance; and yet, armed with the liberty of the press, I will go forth to meet him undismayed. I will attack the mighty fabric of that mightier engine. I will shake down from its height corruption and bury it beneath the ruins of the abuses it was meant to shelter."
—*Richard Brinsley Sheridan, 18th Century Irish dramatist and politician.*

NORTH WALL (LEFT OF WINDOWS)

"The mass of every people must be barbarous where there is no printing, and consequently knowledge is not generally diffused. Knowledge is diffused among our people by newspapers."
—*Samuel Johnson, 18th Century British author and lexicographer.*

"The struggle for freedom of speech has marched hand in hand in the advance of civilization with the struggle for other great human liberties. History teaches that human liberty cannot be secured unless there is freedom to express grievances."
—*From the 1923 decision by the Illinois Supreme Court in an unsuccessful libel suit for $10 million brought against the* Chicago Tribune *by the City of Chicago. The quotation is attributed to Chief Justice Floyd E. Thompson.*

"Congress shall make no law respecting an establishment of religion or prohibiting the free exercise thereof, or abridging the freedom of speech or of the press, or the right of the people peaceably to assemble and to petition the government for a redress of grievances."
—*The First Amendment to the Constitution*

> **"The entire and absolute freedom of the press is essential to the preservation of government on the basis of a free constitution."**
>
> —*Daniel Webster*

NORTH WALL (RIGHT OF WINDOWS)
"No mission too difficult; no sacrifice too great."—*Motto of the U.S. Army First Division, World War I.*

"Take her down!"—*Order given by the fatally wounded Navy commander Howard W. Gilmore on Feb. 7, 1943, as a sinking Japanese gunboat attacked his submarine in the southwest Pacific. Though seriously damaged, the sub returned safely to port. Gilmore was posthumously awarded the Medal of Honor.*

"I want the *Tribune* to continue to be after I am gone as it has been under my directions: an advocate of political and moral progress, and in all things to follow the line of common sense."—*Joseph Medill,* Chicago Tribune *editor, written in 1899, the year of his death.*

EAST WALL (LEFT OF MAP)
"The entire and absolute freedom of the press is essential to the preservation of government on the basis of a free constitution."—*Daniel Webster, statesman and orator, in a speech to the U.S. Senate, March 7, 1850.*

"The nearer you are to the enemy the nearer you are to God."—*Robert R. McCormick,* Chicago Tribune *editor and publisher, en route to Cantigny, France, in 1918, exhorting his troops before battle.*

"Give me liberty or give me death!"—*Patrick Henry, Revolutionary War patriot, orator and statesman.*

EAST WALL (RIGHT OF MAP)
"Newspapers are the sentinels of the liberties of our country."—*Benjamin Rush, member of the Continental Congress and a signer of the Declaration of Independence.*

"Let it be impressed upon your minds, let it be instilled into your children, that the liberty of the press is the palladium of all civil, political and religious rights of freemen."—*"Junius," 18th Century pamphleteer.*

SOUTH WALL (LEFT OF WINDOWS)
"A free press stands as one of the great interpreters between the government and the people. To allow it to be fettered is to fetter ourselves."—*An opinion handed down on Feb. 11, 1936, by Associate Justice George Sutherland and concurred in unanimously by the U.S. Supreme Court in the case of Grossjean vs. The American Press.*

"The newspaper is an institution developed by modern civilization to present the news of the day, to foster commerce and industry, to inform and lead public opinion, and to furnish that check upon government which no constitution has ever been able to provide."—*Robert R. McCormick,* Chicago Tribune *editor and publisher.*

SOUTH WALL (RIGHT OF WINDOWS)
"And ye shall know the truth, and the truth shall make you free."—*The Gospel of St. John, Chapter 8, Verse 32.*

"The liberty of opinion keeps governments themselves in due subjection to their duties."—*Thomas Erskine, Lord Chancellor of England in the first decade of the 19th Century.*

"Our liberty depends on the freedom of the press and that can not be limited without being lost."—*Thomas Jefferson, third president of the United States and chief framer of the Declaration of Independence.*

"To the press alone, checkered as it is with abuses, the world is indebted for all the triumphs which have been gained by reason and humanity over error and oppression."—*James Madison, fourth president of the United States.*

NORTH ELEVATOR LOBBY
"I cannot assent to that view, if it be meant that the legislature may impair or abridge the rights of a free press and of free speech whenever it thinks that the public welfare required that to be done. The public welfare cannot override constitutional privileges, and if the rights of free speech and a free press are, in their essence, attributes of national citizenship, as I think they are, then neither Congress nor any state, since the adoption of the 14th Amendment, can,

by legislative enactments or by judicial action, impair or abridge them."
—*From a decision by John Marshall Harlan, associate justice of the U.S. Supreme Court from 1877 to 1911.*

"But what more oft, in nations grown corrupt, And by their vices brought to servitude, Than to love bondage more than liberty—Bondage with ease than strenuous liberty—And to despise, or envy, or suspect, Whom God hath of His special favour raised As their deliverer?"
—*From "Samson Agonistes," by 17th Century British poet John Milton.*

"Where there is a free press the governors must live in constant awe of the opinions of the governed."—*Thomas Babington Macaulay, 19th Century British essayist, historian, poet and statesman.*

"We in the United States will enjoy freedom of the press just so long as we protect and defend it from attacks by the executive, by the courts, by the legislatures, and by the other powerful arms of government. Government was our servant under the philosophy of our forefathers on which this nation was founded. In all the rest of the world, government is the master of the people. Government, like fire, can be a dutiful servant but a destructive master. If we want to keep liberty it is up to us to make government serve us and never let it become our master."
—*Robert R. McCormick,* Chicago Tribune *editor and publisher.*

○ SOUTH ELEVATOR LOBBY
"The constitutional right of free speech has been declared to be the same in peace and in war. In peace, too, men may differ widely as to what loyalty to our country demands; and an intolerant majority, swayed by passion or by fear, may be prone in the future, as it has often been in the past, to stamp as disloyal, opinions with which it disagrees."
—*Louis D. Brandeis, associate justice of the U.S. Supreme Court from 1916 to 1939.*

"Without freedom of thought there can be no such thing as wisdom; and no such thing as public liberty without freedom of speech; which is the right of every man as far as by it he does not hurt or control the right of another; and this is the only check it ought to suffer and the only bounds it ought to know . . . Whoever would over-

throw the liberty of a nation must begin by subduing the freeness of speech: a thing terrible to public traitors."—*Benjamin Franklin, American statesman, diplomat, author, scientist and inventor.*

"I do not agree with a word you say, but I will defend to the death your right to say it."—*Attributed to Francois Marie Arouet de Voltaire, 18th Century French philosopher, historian, dramatist and essayist.*

NATHAN HALE LOBBY

```
ELEVATORS


                              SECURITY DESK
         E
       N ✦ S
         W



ENTRANCE
```

▪ SOUTH WALL
○ "Let the people know the facts and the country will be safe."
—*Abraham Lincoln, 16th president of the United States.*

"Make no little plans; they have no magic to stir men's blood."—*Daniel Burnham, 1846-1912, Chicago architect and city planning pioneer.*

▪ NORTH WALL
○ "A good newspaper, I suppose, is a nation talking to itself."
—*Arthur Miller, 20th Century American playwright.*

"Our whole constitutional heritage rebels at the thought of giving government the power to control men's minds."
—*Thurgood Marshall, associate justice of the U.S. Supreme Court from 1967 to 1991.*

"The truth does not change according to our ability to stomach it."
—*Flannery O'Connor, 20th Century American novelist.*

"A free press can of course be good or bad but, most certainly, without freedom it will never be anything but bad."—*Albert Camus, 20th Century French philosopher.*

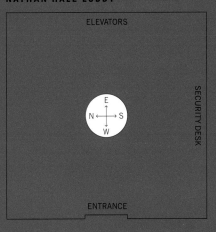

NO MISSION TOO DIFFICULT NO SACRIFICE TOO GREAT "
FIRST DIVISION MOTTO

" TAKE HER DOWN !"
HOWARD GILMORE

" I WANT THE TRIBUNE TO CONTINUE TO BE AFTER I AM GONE AS IT HAS BEEN UNDER MY DIRECTIONS AN ADVOCATE OF POLITICAL AND MORAL PROGRESS AND IN ALL THINGS TO FOLLOW THE LINE OF COMMON SENSE."
JOSEPH MEDILL

OUR LIBERTY DEPENDS ON THE FREEDOM OF THE PRESS AND THAT CAN NOT BE LIMITED WITHOUT BEING LOST.
THOMAS JEFFERSON

CHAPTER SIX

The View from the Top

One of the most thrilling things about a skyscraper is the way it lifts the visitor up and out of the ordinary world along the street, opening stunning vistas of the city around it. That certainly describes the upper reaches of Tribune Tower, where 24th-floor executive offices, including those of former *Chicago Tribune* co-editors and co-publishers Robert R. McCormick and Joseph M. Patterson, are now meeting rooms in a Tribune conference center. But these rooms and the now-closed Tribune Tower observatory on the 25th floor are about much more than eye-popping views. They echo, and in many ways reinforce, Tribune Tower's identity as a secular shrine.

Consider the room leading to the offices where McCormick and Patterson once worked; originally it was the Tribune Company board of directors room and later a secretary's office. The long, narrow space, located between the offices of the co-editors, is crowned by a vaulted, coffered ceiling of ornately carved, dark mahogany. The room resembles a mini-cathedral; there even are little wood closets, tucked in the corners, that suggest confessionals.

A PRESS BARON'S LAIR

Tribune editor and publisher Robert R. McCormick worked in palatial quarters on Tribune Tower's 24th floor. Near the window of his office are an Italian Baroque-style marble table and an American walnut desk chair that is like a throne. The room is now part of a Tribune Company conference center.

HISTORIC HEARTH

The fireplace in McCormick's office is appropriately monumental given the grand scale of the office. Its limestone surface is inscribed with the Colonel's thoughts about the role that a newspaper plays in modern society.

For all the grandeur of McCormick's office, it is never grandiose. Just as in the rest of the Tower, there are enough human-scaled details to prevent the space from being overbearing.

Just off this room, McCormick's office is nothing less than lordly. At one end, there is a monumental fireplace; at the other is an Italian Baroque-style marble table. The American walnut desk chair behind the table is massive and impressive, not unlike a throne. The atmosphere of the office, with its paneled, dark pine walls, is positively baronial, as if the occupant were a king surveying his realm.

The Colonel certainly knew how to play the part and, on occasion, he did so with great mirth. So fine was the joinery of the paneled walls in his lair that visitors trying to leave often had difficulty finding the door. It didn't help that there were no doorknobs. As legend has it, McCormick would mischievously let them squirm as they pressed their hands against the wood in a futile search for a way out. Eventually, after he had had his fun, McCormick would press a button beneath his desk, the elusive door would open, and the embarrassed guest would make a quick exit.

For all the grandeur of McCormick's office, it is never grandiose. Just as in the rest of the Tower, there are enough human-scaled—and, in this case, highly personal—details to prevent the space from being overbearing. One, found in the plaster ceiling, depicts a scroll and key, symbolizing the fraternal organization to which McCormick belonged when he was a student at Yale University. Another, a cannon, also seen in the ceiling, represents his military service during World War I.

Patterson's quarters are every bit as jaw-dropping, though their magnificence has been compromised somewhat by a modern conference table. The

In the 1920s, visitors paid a quarter for a bird's-eye view of downtown Chicago and Lake Michigan from the Tribune Tower observatory (left). The Tower's lookout points also included a terrace (above) a few floors below the observatory from which visitors could peer out at the skyline.

offices of both editors, incidentally, had emergency escape hatches that allowed them to climb hidden stairs to a mezzanine level above the 24th floor. (On the original blueprints, these passages were labeled "file rooms.") It is not known if McCormick and Patterson ever felt the need to use the stairs.

As impressive as the editors' offices are, the former 25th-floor observatory easily tops them when measured by the yardstick of spatial drama. In contrast to today's observatories, which are sealed, air-conditioned lookout points where tourists peer through glass walls, this one is an outdoor, naturally ventilated space that allowed visitors to glimpse magnificent views of Lake Michigan and the Michigan Avenue bridge district through the Tower's Gothic tracery. Even better, they could walk beneath the Tower's flying buttresses, seeing the buttresses frame the sky as well as nearby skyscrapers such as the Wrigley Building.

Still, when it comes to observatories, being the tallest matters the most. The Tower's lookout point was closed in the late 1950s as a result of competition from the observatory at the Prudential Building, which was itself put out of business in later decades by the observatories at Sears Tower and the John Hancock Center.

If today's observatories merely try to entertain the visitor, with high-tech gadgets and other gimmicks, the Tribune's attempted to inform and uplift. Its walls are still inscribed with quotations including a tribute from McCormick to his World War I compatriots in the U.S. Army's legendary First Infantry Division, as well as Abraham Lincoln's entire Gettysburg Address.

VEIL OF STONE
The Tower's Gothic tracery frames a view of the Wrigley Building and, beyond it, the Loop skyline.

CHAPTER SEVEN

New Designs for New Media

Since the 1925 opening of Tribune Tower, Tribune Company has constructed new buildings for new forms of communication. That is as true in the 21st Century, with the explosion of interactive media and the Internet, as it was in the 20th, when radio and then television changed the way that information is disseminated. In a sense, then, the story has come full circle. The new home of Tribune Interactive is located in the pressroom of the old *Chicago Tribune* printing plant, the original Tribune Company building on North Michigan Avenue.

For architects, these projects have posed a challenge: How to embrace the future while not letting go of the past? In each case, the designers have attempted to create visual connections to Tribune Tower while taking their buildings —and Tribune Company—in new directions.

The result is an urban complex, originally known as Tribune Square, that speaks to both continuity and change. Just as in 1925, it is a vital information hub for the Chicago area and the Midwest.

THE TRIBUNE COMPLEX

The Tribune complex on Michigan Avenue has grown in response to the changing needs of Tribune Company and the changing nature of American journalism. Below, an archival photograph shot from the southeast shows the four buildings that make up the complex.

TRIBUNE TOWER
Finished 1925, 36 stories tall. Includes offices of Tribune Company, the *Chicago Tribune* and tenants of Tribune Company.

WGN RADIO BUILDING
Completed 1935, four stories tall. Originally housed radio studios, later offices of *Chicago's American* and *Chicago Today* newspapers. Now home to Tribune Company and *Chicago Tribune* offices, as well as the new McCormick Tribune Freedom Museum.

WGN TELEVISION BUILDING
Finished 1950, ranges from 8 to 11 stories. Initially included television studios; now home to offices of Tribune Company, the *Chicago Tribune* and tenants of Tribune Company.

PRINTING PLANT
Completed 1920, six stories tall. First Tribune Company building on Michigan Avenue. Southern facade refaced in Indiana limestone in 1964 in conjunction with the building of Pioneer Court plaza south of Tribune Tower. Now houses Tribune Company, *Chicago Tribune*, WGN Radio offices and headquarters of Tribune Interactive.

RADIO DAYS

In 1935, workers put finishing touches on the exterior of Tribune Company's new radio building just north of Tribune Tower. The prominently displayed Gothic letters in the facade—W, G and N—stand for the radio station's call letters, which were an abbreviation of the *Tribune's* designation of itself as the World's Greatest Newspaper. That label was a fixture on the newspaper's masthead from 1911 to 1977.

WGN RADIO BUILDING 441-445 N. Michigan Ave.—Built during the Great Depression and representing the growing popularity of radio, this four-story, $600,000 structure represents a simplified version of Tribune Tower's ornate, neo-Gothic style. It was completed in 1935, at a time when American families listened to Franklin D. Roosevelt's radio "fireside chats." The designers were the same team responsible for the Tower—John Mead Howells and Raymond M. Hood, both of New York City—and their associate, J. Andre Fouilhoux. Assisting them was Leo Weissenborn, Tribune Company staff architect. Along with Tribune Tower, the WGN Radio Building flanks the Nathan Hale Court, a plaza that takes its name from a bronze sculpture of the Revolutionary War patriot.

Reflecting a shift in taste toward streamlined forms, the main part of the WGN Radio Building has considerably less decoration than Tribune Tower. Still, the design matches the skyscraper's limestone cladding and has memorable flourishes of its own, including an ornate Gothic entrance set far back from North Michigan Avenue. Originally, the radio station's call letters—"W," "G" and "N"—appeared in Gothic style, several feet high, on the building's exterior. They echoed the *Chicago Tribune's* designation of itself as "The World's Greatest Newspaper," which was a fixture on the newspaper's masthead from 1911 to 1977.

The WGN Radio Building housed six radio studios and a 588-seat theater from which programs were broadcast. This Art Deco showplace was designed

A spiral of aluminum plates, each like a piece of paper stamped with an individual's story expressing a First Amendment freedom, will form a two-story sculpture suspended from the rotunda ceiling at the center of the Freedom Museum. Its designers, Peter Bernheim and Amy Larimer of San Diego, won an international juried art competition for the project in 2005. Their sculpture is titled "12151791," recognizing the First Amendment's ratification date.

by Ernest Grunsfeld Jr., architect of the Adler Planetarium; he won a nationwide competition for the project, which offered a $2,500 first prize.

In 1961, WGN Radio joined WGN-TV in a modern, two-story building at 2501 W. Bradley Place on Chicago's Northwest Side. The architects of the $3 million project were Graham, Anderson, Probst & White of Chicago. At the same time, the WGN Radio Building was remodeled as the new home of the newspaper *Chicago's American,* which Tribune Company had purchased in 1956. Chicago architects Holabird & Root and Burgee altered the facade, removing the Gothic letters and inserting windows into the upper stories, which originally were covered in stone. In 1969, *Chicago's American,* an afternoon newspaper, was renamed *Chicago Today.*

Since *Chicago Today* ceased publication in 1974, the WGN Radio Building has housed offices of Tribune Company and the *Chicago Tribune.* WGN Radio returned to the Tribune complex in 1986, occupying the southern side of Tribune Tower and part of the former *Chicago Tribune* printing plant.

In 2006, the McCormick Tribune Freedom Museum will open on the first and second floors of the WGN Radio Building. Designed by VOA Associates of Chicago, the interactive museum will provide visitors opportunities to question, challenge and debate the application and cost of freedom. It also will commemorate the 50th anniversary of the McCormick Tribune Foundation, a charitable trust formed in 1955 after the death of former *Chicago Tribune* editor and publisher Robert R. McCormick.

STRAIGHT SHOOTERS
The WGN Radio Building hosted many popular radio programs. This photograph shows the principals in the cast of "Tom Mix and his Straight Shooters," which was one of radio's oldest and most beloved serials for children.

THE RISE OF TV

This 1949 photo shows the new WGN-TV Building standing behind the WGN Radio Building. The marquee in front of the radio building has been updated to reflect the importance of TV.

FUN AND GAMES
Young students from Resurrection Lutheran parish school sitting in a corridor of Tribune Tower wait to enter the WGN-TV studio to see the antics of Uncle Ned, Uncle Bob and Aunt Dodie on "Lunch Time Theater" in 1960.

WGN-TV BUILDING If the first WGN building alongside Tribune Tower reflected the emergence of radio, the second spoke to the power of television—and to the continuing move toward simple, abstract forms in architecture. Completed in 1950, as television sets found their way into the nation's living rooms, it was designed by Harrison, Fouilhoux and Abramovitz of New York City; Howells; and Weissenborn.

Built mainly to house studio and office space for WGN-TV, the $8 million addition also accommodated new presses and newsroom facilities for the *Chicago Tribune*. It is located along the north wall of the Tower and extends behind the WGN Radio Building before continuing eastward toward Lake Michigan. Ranging from 8 to 11 stories, the WGN-TV Building is similar in style to the WGN Radio Building, with limestone cladding, flattened piers that emphasize vertical lines, and a modest amount of Gothic decoration. It makes a graceful transition between the soaring Tribune Tower and the much lower WGN Radio Building.

The WGN-TV Building incorporated new technologies, notably air conditioning and fluorescent lighting, that came into wide use after World War II. Floors were placed on the same level as those of existing Tribune buildings to enable employees, tenants and visitors to move easily throughout the complex.

Currently, the WGN-TV Building houses a portion of the *Chicago Tribune* newsroom, Tribune Tower tenants and Tribune corporate offices. One of its former studios, Studio 7A, is an auditorium called Campbell Hall.

Bridging the identities of the original printing plant of the *Chicago Tribune* and the computer technology of the 21st Century, the new headquarters of Tribune Interactive retains features of the old pressroom, such as the glazed tile that covered structural steel columns. It also incorporates the Tribune Fitness Center and a conference and training center.

TRIBUNE INTERACTIVE HEADQUARTERS Located in the cavernous former pressroom of Tribune Tower, this subterranean interior symbolizes the growing importance of interactive media and the Internet. It retains certain features of the old pressroom, such as the glazed tile that covered structural steel columns. As a result, the Tribune Interactive headquarters offers a pointed contrast between the muscular, industrial look of the early 20th Century and the sleek, high-tech aesthetic of the early 21st Century.

Designed by Chicago-based Perkins & Will, with McClier of Chicago serving as associate architects, the $22 million, 85,000-square-foot facility incorporates open work stations as well as the Tribune Fitness Center and a conference and training center.

To bring natural light into the space, a ground-level loading dock was refitted with glass walls. Inside, steel bridges slice across the three-story main room. Safety railings for the bridges carry power and data lines. Around a three-story central area, glass-walled conference rooms are stacked in groups of three known as "towers." These buildings-within-a-building provide focal points while recalling the vertical forms of Tribune Tower.

In 2002, the Tribune Interactive headquarters won a National Honor Award for interior architecture from the American Institute of Architects. It represents the latest example of how Tribune Tower embodies the changing character of American journalism, as well as the highest standards of architecture and design.

STILL ON TRACK
Architects retained old narrow-gauge railroad tracks, once used for transporting massive rolls of newsprint in the *Chicago Tribune* pressroom, in the floor of the Tribune Interactive offices.

International Standard Book Number: 0-615-11565-9 (paper)
Library of Congress Card Number: 00-105137

ABOUT THE CONTRIBUTORS

Blair Kamin, who provided the commentary for this book, joined the *Chicago Tribune* as a reporter in 1987 and became the newspaper's architecture critic in 1992. He received the 1999 Pulitzer Prize for criticism for a body of work highlighted by a series of articles on Chicago's lakefront. His other prizes include the George Polk Award for criticism and the Institute Honor for Collaborative Achievement from the American Institute of Architects. A native of New Jersey, Kamin is a graduate of Amherst College and the Yale University School of Architecture.

Bob Fila, major photographer for this book, began his newspaper career as a copy boy for *Chicago's American* and has been a *Chicago Tribune* photographer since 1970. He was part of the *Chicago Tribune* team that won the 2001 Pulitzer Prize for explanatory reporting for its profile of the chaotic American air traffic system. He is the recipient of numerous other awards, including Illinois and Chicago Photographer of the Year. Born in Chicago, Fila studied photography at the Winona School of Professional Photography and Chicago's Ray Vogue School of Photography.

BLAIR KAMIN

BOB FILA

Design: Pressley Jacobs, Chicago
Printing: Active Graphics, Inc., Chicago

Images:
Chris Walker, *Chicago Tribune*, stones photos on pages 19-26, lobby photo on page 35
Steve Hall, Hedrich Blessing, page 51
Cover photos and all other non-archival photography by Bob Fila

ACKNOWLEDGMENTS

This book would not have been possible without the encouragement and support of Jack Fuller, former president of Tribune Publishing Company, and Scott Smith, his successor. Former *Chicago Tribune* editor Howard Tyner provided excellent suggestions. Faith Brown, formerly of Tribune Corporate Relations, served as project manager for the first edition; Jeff Reiter, from the same department, assisted with the second edition. Nancy Watkins from the *Chicago Tribune* was an invaluable copy editor for both editions.

Background information and archival research were provided by Al Gramzinski, former director/property management, Tribune Company; Mary Jo Mandula, director/property management, Tribune Company; John Dewey, building operations manager, Tribune Company; Ron Grossman, staff reporter, *Chicago Tribune*; Philip Hamp, principal, Vinci/Hamp Architects, Inc.; Eric Gillespie, director of the Robert R. McCormick Research Center; Walter Arnold, Chicago stone carver; the late Michael Camille, professor of art history, University of Chicago; and Katherine Solomonson, associate professor, University of Minnesota.